SUCH MEN ARE DANGEROUS

SUCH MEN ARE DANGEROUS

LAWRENCE BLOCK

Carroll & Graf Publishers, Inc.
New York

Copyright © 1969 by Paul Kavanagh

Published by arrangement with the author and the author's agent,
Knox Burger Associates, Inc.

First Carroll & Graf edition 1993

Carroll & Graf Publishers, Inc.
260 Fifth Avenue
New York, NY 10001

ISBN 0-7867-0047-5

Manufactured in the United States of America

SUCH MEN ARE DANGEROUS

ONE

THE DESK MEN at the Agency run to type. They are all an inch or two over average. They wear dark suits, white shirts, striped ties. They drink scotch and water or bourbon and water or, in the summer, vodka collinses. They work out once a week at a gym, usually handball or squash. They smile a lot, but not quite enough to get on your nerves. You wouldn't mistake them for sales managers or purchasing agents, but might think they were personnel men, which, come to think of it, is close. If you'd been around them much, you'd place them right off. This isn't the liability it might seem; they don't operate under cover, hardly ever leave Washington, and so it doesn't matter a hell of a lot who knows what they are.

This particular one was no more than a couple of percentage points off the standard. He was a little bonier than most, and I'd guess his weekly exercise was cross-country running. He shook hands firmly, looked me right in the eyes when he talked, and had a voice that was resonant with sincerity and definition of purpose. None of this means anything, ever.

He said, "Sorry we've taken so long processing you, Mr.

1

Kavanagh. You know how it is, the mills of God and the wheels of bureaucracy.''

"No problem.'' Nor had it been. They had me staying at the Doulton and they were covering the tab, and three weeks of good food and plush surroundings had not been hard to take. Waiting did not bother me; patience is as much a part of the life as action.

"I hope you've enjoyed Washington?''

"Sure.''

"And they've made you comfortable here?''

"No complaints.''

"Good.''

I waited for him to say something, and it took me a minute to realize that he wasn't going to. I thought of out-staring him. Pointless; it was my hotel room, but it was his town, so we would play it by his rules. He was waiting for me, which meant he had an answer for me, which meant there was a question I was supposed to ask.

I smiled with as much warmth as he deserved and asked three. "Well,'' I said, "where do I go and who do I see and when do I start?''

His face clouded on cue. "Good question,'' he said. "The thing is, Paul, that I'm afraid there's nothing open right now, nothing that's your sort of thing, not at the moment. The way things stand at the present time—''

"Wait a minute.''

He stopped, looked at me.

"Let's start over,'' I said. "I didn't trot on down to Washington with a question mark on my forehead. You people called me, remember? You asked me if I'd like to join the team. I said I didn't have anything better to do, and it sounded good, and I came here and went through the inter-view routine and took the tests, and didn't make any waves, and three weeks disappeared, and now—''

"You'll be paid for your time.''

"Oh, the hell with that. If my time's not worth anything I don't care whether or not I'm paid for it.'' I got out of the comfy chair and walked across the deep carpet toward the window with the overpowering view of our nation's Capitol. I got halfway there and turned around. "Look, you don't mean that there's no job open. There's always a job open. What you mean is that somebody who wanted Paul Kavanagh changed his mind during the past three weeks. What I'd like to know is why."

"Paul—"

"I want to know, and I want you to tell me. Maybe you want to go someplace else because your people bugged the room. That's fine, but—"

"Don't be silly. We didn't bug the room."

"Then we're all in trouble, because there's been a pebble mike in the light socket since I checked in, and—"

He got to his feet. "It's ours."

"Of course it is. Look, Dattner—"

"George."

"George. George, I know the game. I honestly do. I've played it and I know how it goes. Understood?"

"All right."

"So I'm not asking you to reconsider, because in the first place you didn't make the decision and in the second place these decisions aren't reconsidered. I know all this. Okay?" He nodded. "All I want is an explanation. Somewhere in the past three weeks somebody's mind changed. I want to know why. I know my record over the past ten years. Laos, Vietnam, Cambodia—I got good marks right down the line, and I know it, and there's nothing that could have turned up recently that wasn't on my sheet all along. Right?"

"Go on."

"Well, what else is there? My civilian record? I don't have one. Family? They were all lifelong Republicans except for a maverick uncle who voted for Truman in '48. They're all dead now anyway. College? I never signed a petition or joined a political group. I played football and kept up a B-minus average. Somebody wanted me to run for student council once but I didn't have the time. Or the inclination.

After graduation I had a tryout for the Steelers. I was too light for pro ball. In August my father died, and in September I enlisted in the Army. I made squad leader in basic and I went Airborne because I was scared of heights and didn't want to admit it. Half the guys I knew were there for the same reason. The rest wanted to get killed, and some of them made it. Then I was over there for ten years, and you know about that. I could have stayed ten more years, but everybody gets tired of jungles sooner or later. I did, and I came home, and I'm here, and—''

I turned away from him, chopped it off in the middle of a sentence and walked over to the window. I was annoyed with myself. The occasion didn't warrant that sort of speech. I was letting myself get angry. There are times when it's worthwhile to do this, times when a self-induced emotional buildup helps you function better, but this wasn't that sort of time.

I looked at Washington until the tension went away, then turned to Dattner. George. He asked if there was anything around to drink. I had a bottle of reasonably good Scotch in the bureau. I told him no, but I could call Room Service if he wanted. He told me not to bother.

I went over and sat down again. He was still standing. "Your turn," I said.

"Pardon me?"

"Your turn. I talked, and now you can talk. I've been out of uniform for four months and it's inconceivable that I could have done anything suspicious in that time. I haven't consorted with any communists or foreign agents. I haven't consorted with anybody, I—The hell with it. It's your turn, friend. I'm either a security risk or an incompetent. You're going to tell me which I am, and how you people found me out.''

He gave me a long searching glance, and then his eyes moved momentarily to the overhead light fixture where they had planted their little toy. I think he did this on purpose.

"I've already told you all I'm authorized to," he said.

"I realize that.''

"So . . ."

It took a second, but I picked up my cue. "I won't let it lie," I said, cooperatively. "If you go out of here now I'll make waves until I find out what it's all about. Ask enough people and you get an answer. I can ask my congressman, I can ask some reporters—"

A quick grin showed on his face but not in his voice. "That's not good," he said. "I don't . . . Paul, if I tell you what I know, will you let it ride?"

"If it makes sense."

"I don't know if it will or not. It makes sense, but it might not make sense to you."

"Try me. Incompetent? Security risk? What am I?"

"A little of both."

The anger came, an instantaneous tightening of the muscles in my legs and abdomen. I was ready for it, I knew it was coming, I was prepped in advance to keep a lid on it, but even so I suspect some of it showed. But I didn't reveal it to the little bug on the ceiling. When I spoke, I made the words offhand, casual.

"You'd better tell me about it," I said.

And he did.

I'd been right—it was nothing in my service record, nothing in the college years or the years before, nothing in my family background. It was not, in fact, anything I had done. It was what I *was*.

"We've spent three weeks on you," Dattner said. "We know more about you than you do, but that won't surprise you. Part of our investigation has been your past history, and that's good, just as you said. We knew that before we contacted you, before we invited you to Washington. If your record wasn't perfect you never would have heard from us. Of course we went over it again, but nothing bad turned up.

"Your record was only half of it, though. The rest of our investigation was concerned with what you are now, not what you've been and done in the past. That's where the interviews came in, and the testing. There was a purpose to all those forms you filled out. Know much about testing?''

"Just that I took enough tests to last me the rest of my life."

"Uh-huh. Know what they were designed to show?"

I shrugged. "Whether or not I'm crazy, I suppose. The political tests were pretty obvious, though I would think that a person could fake his way through them—"

"Not as easily as you might think."

"Maybe not. I'm no expert. The others, let me think. There were physical tests which I'm sure I passed, everything from health and coordination to weapons and unarmed combat skills. I know I did well on that. And there was the psychological bit, questions like do I think little men are following me. A year ago I would have said yes, because a whole platoon of little brown men *were* following me, but that's off the point, isn't it?"

He didn't smile. I guess it wasn't funny.

"I suppose that test would show up personality problems. Homosexuality, that sort of thing. Or out-and-out nuttiness. And what else was there? IQ tests, on which I must have done fairly well, and tests to measure spatial relations and mechanical aptitude. One time they gave me a faucet to put back together, a water faucet. If that's what kept me out—"

"No."

"Because I've always had my heart set on being a plumber, and—"

He lit a cigarette. "There were other tests," he said. "Sometimes you were being tested when you didn't know it. Your emotional reactions when you were kept waiting, that sort of thing. Psychologists are a sneaky bunch." He looked around for an ashtray, and I got up and found him one. "Matter of fact," he went on, "a psychologist could explain all of this better than I can. But I'll talk to you and they wouldn't, so don't get mad at me if I sound a little vague. It's not my province."

I told him that was fair enough. He said all he could do was give me the gist of it in layman's language, and I said layman's language was all I could understand. He sat back and put out his cigarette and I waited, not entirely certain I wanted to hear what he was going to tell me.

"Personality tests," he said finally. "They're considerably more sophisticated than you may realize. The one you mentioned with the questions about little men following you, for example. That's the MMPI—"

"Which means what?"

"Minnesota Multi-Phasic Something-or-Other. It can spotlight a great many emotional conditions ranging from hysteria and paranoia to I don't know what. Even when you know how it works it's hard to cheat it. It's been in general use for years—"

"I took it two months ago."

"Uh-huh. Job application?"

I nodded. "I applied for a dozen different things. Corporate executive positions. Some companies wanted me, but nobody offered me anything that excited me. One company gave me that test."

"Did they offer you a job?"

"Haven't heard from them yet."

"I don't think they'll hire you."

"Really?"

He nodded. "Your MMPI profile won't be what they're looking for."

"What am I? Hysterical or paranoid?"

"Neither. But you're not a company man, either."

"Go on."

He thought for a moment. "I don't really have the vocabulary to make this work," he said finally. "There were, oh, I don't know how many tests. It would be pointless to go over each one and explain what it did and how you did on it. I can just sort of sum up what we found out. And I can tell you that the syndrome, the personality pattern that showed up, is not unusual. Not for a person of your background.

"I said before that you were a security risk and an incompetent. For a second I thought you were going to swing on me." I admitted that the impulse had been fairly strong. "Maybe I can make it clearer for you, then. Our tests indicate that you are not highly motivated in any particular direction. In other words, there's nothing you want very much. You don't want a million dollars, you're not hungry for power, you're not burning up with some social or political cause—"

"Is this bad?"

"Let me finish. What it boils down to, really, is that nothing matters to you very much, nothing beyond doing the job at hand, living a reasonably comfortable life, and staying alive."

"So that means I'm crazy?"

"No. It might mean you're too sane."

"You lost me."

"I was afraid I would." He sighed. "From what I've said so far, you would seem to shape up as a perfect prospect for us." The same thought had occurred to me. "You'll do what you're ordered to do, you won't let personal ambition turn you off the track, you don't have any obvious weakness that an enemy could exploit. So far it sounds like a perfect description of one of our operatives."

"Or a robot."

"Remember that you said that, it's relevant." He took out another cigarette but didn't light this one. "To go on— you've got the lack of motive that fits the right pattern. But our men have something else, something that makes them function competently, something that keeps them from being security risks. It's a deep drive to serve their country."

A dozen things occurred to me at once and I did not say any of them.

"Not because they're born patriots and you're not, Paul. Usually it's not a very pretty reason at all. Some of the time—I'd say a lot of the time, frankly—it's because they're latent homosexuals who have to prove themselves as men. And not always latent, either; some of our best men are, well, forget it."

"Stick to the point."

"Uh-huh. The point, I guess, is that they have to serve *us*. The nation, the Agency itself, it hardly matters which. If they're robots, the controls that make them tick are here in Washington. The Agency fills a vital role in their lives, father or mother or brother or whatever. They will do whatever they are ordered to do."

"And I wouldn't."

"No, you wouldn't. Ten years ago you would have, and now you wouldn't, and that's the difference."

"I don't get it."

"Of course you don't, damn it." He worried his forehead with his fingertips. "All right, let's look at it from another direction. Do you honestly think you would take a black pill?" I stared at him. "A death pill. Cyanide in a hollow tooth, a lethal capsule sewn under your skin, whatever. Say your cover is blown and you're captured and have to undergo interrogation. The only way to prevent the other side from pumping you is to take yourself out of the play. Would you do it?"

"I suppose so."

He shook his head. "If you really think so, you're wrong. I can't prove it to you. It's true, just the same. You wouldn't do it. Nor would you stand up very long under torture. Don't interrupt me, Paul. You would realize even before they really started to hurt you that sooner or later you would talk, and you would know that it made good sense to talk right away and avoid unnecessary pain. And you'd sing like a soprano."

"I can't believe that."

"Should I stop now?"

"Not until you've told me something I can make sense out of."

"All right. Maybe this will help. You wouldn't stand torture and you wouldn't kill yourself for a very good reason. You would work it out in your mind, and you would realize that it just wasn't worth it, that it wouldn't make sense. Why die to keep the Chinese from learning a minor bit of data that probably wouldn't do them a dime's worth of good anyway? Why lose an arm or an eye or a night's sleep and ultimately tell them anyway? And, to take it a half step further, why get killed when you could preserve yourself by turning double agent? Ten years ago you wouldn't have thought those things out. Ten years ago you could have reasoned that a man really could get himself killed jumping out of planes, and that chunk of insight would have kept you out of the paratroops.''

"I'd jump tomorrow. Today, if you want.''

"Because you're not afraid of heights anymore.''

"So?''

"So you're not afraid of heights. So at the same time you've gone through an emotional change. In a sense you've lost something, but there's another way to look at it. You might well say that you've gained something, that you've grown up and learned how to think for yourself.''

"And that's bad?''

"It may be good for you. It's bad for us.''

"Because I've learned to look out for Number One? That's what we did in those jungles, friend. We were a batch of mercenary soldiers doing a job.''

"You re-enlisted and stayed there.''

"I enjoyed it.''

"And then, after ten years, you came back.''

"I stopped enjoying it.''

"Think about it and you'll see there's more to it than that. Oh, hell. You've become a man we can't count on, that's all. Forget the torture bit, forget the black pill you wouldn't take. It goes deeper. It touches points that would be more apt to come up than self-destruction. Suppose we ordered you to go to a hostile country and assassinate a political leader.''

"I'd do it.''

"Agreed—you would do it. Now take it a step further. Suppose we ordered you to go to a neutral country and assassinate a pro-western politician so that the government would launch reprisals against the communists. Your role would be to join the man's staff, become friendly with him, then murder him and frame the communists for it.''

"You people don't do things like that."

He looked at the ceiling. "Let's say we don't. But suppose we decided to one day, and we picked you for the job. And you met the man, and liked him, and decided he was important to the future of his country. Then what?"

I felt trapped. "It's a stupid question," I said.

"Answer it."

"I'd think it over, I'd—"

"You'd think it over. Stop right there. When they told you to mop up a band of Laotian guerrillas, did you stop to figure out just who they were and what they were doing?"

"That's not the same—"

"The hell it's not!" The words came out in what was almost a shout, and he had to force his voice down to its normal volume. This amused me. I was the one who should be flying off the handle. "Sorry," he said. "But it is the same. An effective agent is like an effective soldier. He does what he's told, no more and no less."

"Sometimes a soldier has to use his judgment."

"But only when he's told to. The rest of the time he doesn't have any judgment. He follows orders."

"Like a good German soldier."

"Precisely."

"Like the Light Brigade."

"That's the idea."

"And I wouldn't do that."

"No, Paul. You'd think about it. You'd do a Hamlet, you'd think it over, you'd work it out in your mind. On the most basic level, this would make you inefficient. You'd be too slow, and you'd boggle some assignments. That's serious enough, but you'd do worse than that sooner or later. You'd question policy. You'd reason it out, and there would come a time when you disagreed with a policy, and then you'd either purposely bungle it or else refuse to execute it. You might even come to the careful, rational conclusion that the world would work out better if you helped the other side—"

"Treason, in other words."

"If you like. If I called you a potential traitor ten years ago, you couldn't have taken it so calmly. The word itself, the concept, would have infuriated you. A man who's capable of hearing a word calmly is capable of performing the deed."

"Wait a minute."

"What?"

"Well, I'm not a psychologist either, damn it, but isn't this a little too theoretical? What you're saying is that you can't use anybody with a brain—"

"Wrong. We need intelligence."

"Then what?"

"It's the way the brain is used. We need a man with a short circuit in his brain so that the process of independent thought is bypassed. That sounds ridiculous, but—"

"It does," I agreed. "But the whole thing sounds as though it was worked out by a computer. I don't buy it."

He was smiling, but it was a new smile. "Yes, you do," he said. "You've already bought it. You know what I'm getting at, you accept it, and the only argument you can raise is that it's theoretical, that it doesn't work that way in practice. But you really know better. You poor bastard."

This time he lit the cigarette. "We interview a great many men in your position, men with your track record. We reject a hell of a lot of them, because we've backtracked our failures over the years until we've proved what you've just described as theory. We've analyzed the fuckups and the defectors, we've typed them, and we know how to test our prospects. Know what else we do? We give periodic checks to our own field men. I don't have the figures, but a high percentage of them fail sooner or later. They turn that corner, they conquer the force that made them good to begin with, and somewhere along the line they learn to think. Then we put them on desks in Washington, or retire them altogether."

"Because they can think."

"Yes."

"Because they've grown up, maybe."

"Something like that." The smile again. "They grow up, Paul. They grow up, and they can't tag along with Peter Pan any more. They stop believing in fairies. And then they can't fly. They can't fly."

I went over to the bureau and got out the bottle of Scotch. He didn't bother to remind me that I had denied possession of it a little while ago. I poured two drinks, added water. I asked if he wanted me to call down for ice, but he said it wasn't necessary. I gave him his drink. I took a sip of my own, and I thought that a year or so ago I would have reacted to a conversation like this one by getting very drunk indeed. I thought about getting drunk now, and I realized that there was really no point to it. And it was about then that I began to understand that he was right.

He broke the silence by asking me what I thought about it now. Did I believe him?

"I'll have to think about it."

"Sure. There are two answers—*No* and *I'll have to think about it*. Which means yes."

"Maybe."

And after a while I said, "So what do I do now? Isn't there any slot open with you people where an old philosopher would come in handy?"

"No. First of all, you're not particularly qualified for desk stuff. And whatever you did, you'd want to dictate policy. One way or another."

"So? That means I'm unemployable at thirty-two. Wonderful."

"There are any number of civilian jobs—"

"I thought you said I'd fail their personality tests, too."

"Not everyone gives them. And not every company is looking for what we're looking for. As far as that goes, there's a book on how to beat those tests. They won't beat ours, but they'll get you through the average corporate testing routine."

"As far as that goes, I've had job offers."

"Naturally."

"Some fairly good ones. Decent money, work I can handle—"

"Right."

I studied the rug. "I threw them all away when you people called me. Never gave them a second thought. That's how much they excited me."

"Maybe a business of your own—"

"Sure."

"If you have capital, back pay saved up—"

"I've thought about it. I can't see it."

More silence. He got up and went to the john. I looked at my drink and tried to think of a reason for finishing it. I couldn't. He came back, walked over to the window. It was getting darker outside. He came back and sat down again.

I said, "I suppose I'll sit around on a beach until my money runs out. Then I'll have to take a job."

"Sure."

"Mmmm."

"A lot of fellows with your training, they find work. You must know what I mean."

"Mercenaries?"

"Of course, and don't tell me you haven't considered it. If it's adventure you miss, that's where you'll find it. Africa's not that different from Southeast Asia, is it?"

"Maybe not."

"And the recruiters in Johannesburg and Salisbury don't use the MMPI. Nor do they really expect loyalty. You'd fit."

"On whose side?"

"What's the difference?"

"Oh. That's a point."

Another silence. Then he finished his drink, got abruptly to his feet. "Guess that does it," he said. "I'd have preferred to skip this whole conversation, to tell you the truth. I'm not sure you'd have made much of a stink. A lot of rejects who want answers talk about going to their congressmen or to the press. Not many of them try. But it seemed worthwhile to cool you off. If I told you things you would have just as soon not heard, I'm sorry, but that's how it goes.''

If he was really sorry, I thought, then his days at the Agency were numbered. Then I amended that. He was really sorry, but he'd forget about it the minute he went out the door. Once he stopped being able to forget, then he would be on his way out.

I let him out. We didn't shake hands, although he seemed ready to. I had nothing against him, but I had nothing for him, either. He was just doing his job, right?

TWO

TWO HOURS LATER I boarded a jet for New York, and two hours after that I was in my own room in a hotel on West 44th Street. It was a comedown after the Doulton, but I paid my own bill and I liked it better that way. I went through my mail, which included job offers, requests for interviews, and, from the company which had given me the MMPI, an explanation that they had nothing for me at the moment.

In the morning I walked over to Brentano's and bought a book called *How to Beat Personality Tests*. That was the actual title. I read a little over a third of it before chucking it out. Then I began writing various companies to explain that I couldn't accept a position with them at the present time. I wrote four or five letters before it occurred to me that I could attain the same results just as easily by not writing them at all. I tore up the letters I had written, and I threw them out along with the letters from the companies.

I went to a play one night but left after the first act. It was a comedy, and it's disheartening to be the only person in the audience who isn't laughing. I also went to several movies. I picked up some paperbacks but rarely read one all the way through. The war stories were too inaccurate. The mysteries were a little better, but I didn't much care who done it. The big fat novels with quotes on their covers explaining how they probed with fresh insight into the fabric of modern society, those were the worst of all. I couldn't understand the characters. They were all hung up on trivia, little nothing problems in their careers and marriages. Maybe I might have given a damn if I had had a career or a marriage, but I doubted it. The major point in every book I read seemed to be that people couldn't communicate with one another. I decided they should all study Esperanto, and I threw the books away one after another.

The movies were just as silly, but I didn't have to read them. I could just sit there while they happened.

The rest of the time I didn't do very much at all. There was a television set in my room. I asked them if they could take it out and give me a radio, and they brought me a small AM-FM radio and told me I could keep the television set too. I never turned the tv on. Sometimes I listened to music on the radio, but most of the time I forgot to bother, so I could have lived just as well without it.

I could never think of anybody to call.

One night I picked up a girl in the elevator. Where else would I meet one? This one broke a heel in the elevator, stepping between it and the floor. We got to talking while I freed the heel from the crack, and decided to have dinner together. She went upstairs for new shoes and came back down and I bought her tempura at a Japanese place on the next block. We left our shoes at the door and sat on mats, so I talked about furloughs in Tokyo. She asked if Japanese women were as wonderful as they were supposed to be, which established the program for the evening. I said something about going to a nightclub, and she said she'd have to change, and when we got back to the hotel I found out she was a better girl than I'd suspected. We didn't have to go anywhere first. We went to her room, and she found a bottle and two glasses, and we went to bed.

She was tall, which I like. She had fine legs and a good bottom and small but honest breasts. Brown hair with a lot of red in it, and marvelous skin, and a good face. There was really nothing about her to object to. We kissed a little and hugged a little and went to bed, and the stupid little soldier wouldn't stand at attention.

This had happened only once before, not counting the inevitable occasions when alcohol had unprovoked lechery. Just once in the dim past had the old soldier thrown down his arms, and at the time I had been angry, terrified, ashamed, and hopelessly embarrassed, four emotions which persisted until another night and another girl reassured me that I was still a man.

But this time I was none of those things, and all that really bothered me was the absence of reaction; I was suddenly finding myself not only impotent but evidently resigned to it, and it was the resignation that I objected to.

I offered an excuse, more for her self-esteem than my own. Malaria, I explained; I'd had an attack just two nights ago, and this was a common consequence, an almost inevitable after-effect. I hadn't, and it isn't, but I was so calm and matter-of-fact about it she could hardly fail to believe me. She said we could try some other time, but I felt it was less than gentlemanly to leave her like that. I sort of liked her. So I got down to business with an organ less capricious than the old battle-scarred warrior.

She wanted to return the favor, malaria or no, and it turned out that this was a task at which she was astonishingly adept, so much so that the proper response occurred and I was able to conclude the proceedings according to the usual format. I performed passably if not exceptionally, and if she keeps a diary I don't suppose I deserved much more than a C-plus.

"See," she said later. "I can cure malaria."

"You're better than quinine."

"Maybe I'll become an army nurse."

"Maybe I'll re-enlist."

"Would you believe that I've never done that before? I

didn't think you would. I don't always, though, and when I
do I don't always enjoy it, and—"

"Look, Sharon—"

"What I mean is I rather like you," she said clumsily, a
tear staining her pretty cheek. "Are my cheeks pretty? Seriously, Paul, I tend to carry candor too far. Honesty can be
misleading, don't you think? I'm twenty-nine, I was di-
vorced a little over three years ago. I'm not a tramp, I
wouldn't call me a tramp, but you might, and I don't think I'd
like that."

"Don't be silly."

"All right. I'm a legal secretary in Milwaukee, and this is a
vacation, and it ends Sunday when I fly home. I'm not in love
with anybody right now, including you, although I probably
could be if things worked that way. There are three, no, four
nights between now and Sunday, and if you would like me to
spend them with you I think I would probably like that, and if
you would rather not I think I could survive the inevitable ego
damage. Don't say anything now. This little speech wasn't a
question. It was just so that you would know who I am. I
think people should know each other before they make love a
second time. I also think we should make love a second time.
How does your malaria feel?"

We made love a second time, and my malaria was evidently cured. I raised the C-plus to somewhere around an
A-minus, and it was all very nice indeed. She fell quickly
asleep. I got dressed and went down two floors to my own
room and got undressed and into bed and didn't sleep.

I decided if I saw her for the next four nights that would be
fine, and if I didn't see her ever again that would be fine, too.
It seemed to me that I ought to care one way or the other. I
also realized that she was the first woman I had had since
returning to the States. This also struck me as somehow
remarkable.

When the sun came up I went over to a travel agent on Fifth
Avenue and priced flights to Rhodesia and South Africa.
They came to more than I would have guessed, but money
was no problem. I could have chartered a private plane if I

wanted. Between back pay and government bonds and my mother's insurance, I had close to twenty thousand dollars.

I spent the afternoon at the movies. Afterward I tried to decide whether or not I should see Sharon again. It was impossible to decide which way I would prefer it, so I tried to determine which would be better for her, whether she would be more upset if my permanent goodbye came now or in four days. Then I decided that it was impossible to say, and that, as far as that went, I didn't really give a damn whether I upset her or not, at which point I decided to think about something else.

I went somewhere for a cup of coffee. I thought about becoming a white mercenary somewhere in darkest Africa, and all I could come up with was that it was something to do, which struck me as the strongest possible argument for and against it, all at once. The one thing I wanted was something to do, and the one thing I didn't want was something to do. I decided that George Dattner had not told me the whole truth. The MMPI had obviously revealed that I was psychotic.

I went back to the hotel. That night I took Sharon to dinner at a steakhouse on Third Avenue. Afterward we went to a jazz club and drank something sweet with tequila in it, I forget what. Then to her room, where we both got A-plus.

The next day I went through the yellow pages until I found a psychiatrist with whom I could get an appointment the following day. That night Sharon and I saw a play, went to a kosher delicatessen for a late supper, and then made love.

The following day there was a new movie I wanted to see, so I skipped the appointment with the psychiatrist. I didn't call him. When I got back to the hotel there was a message from his office. I threw it away. Sharon had dinner with an old friend. I met her afterward, and we picked up a copy of *Cue* and couldn't think of a thing we wanted to do, so we went to her room. She said the hotel staff seemed to be delighted with our romance, and I said maybe they wanted to use us in their advertising. We went to bed, and I sat up the whole night trying to figure out how it could be possible for me to spend so much time making ecstatic love with such a superb girl without enjoying it. I neither looked forward to it nor relished its memory. It was something I did, like taking breaths.

The next day was Sharon's last, so we went to an expensive restaurant and an expensive nightclub and sat through an expensive floorshow, neither of us daring to disappoint the other by admitting how boring it all was. We sat through a dance team and a singer. When the comic came on I noticed that she wasn't laughing either. I said, "Why don't we get out of here?" and she said, "I thought you'd never ask." I put too much money on the table and we got up and walked right out, passing directly in front of the bandstand just as the poor clown was coming to a punchline. He proved he could be rude, too, by abandoning his joke and insulting us. Sharon told him to fuck himself.

Outside she told me she couldn't quite believe she'd said that. "Forget it," I said. "Right now he's telling them it's the best offer he's had all night, and everybody's laughing nervously. Let's get some coffee."

Over coffee she talked about Milwaukee. She mentioned her daughter, of whom I had not previously heard, and said she was staying with her mother, whom she hadn't mentioned either. She also talked about her boss; the implication seemed to be that he was married, and that she was sleeping with him, and doing so largely because he was there. She never quite said this, but I wouldn't have inferred it if she hadn't wanted me to.

Then we went up to her room, and told each other that the floorshow probably hadn't been as bad as it seemed to us, and then we went to bed, and neither of us could get in the mood. I made us a couple of drinks and we talked.

I came fairly close to opening up. I talked a little about the years in Special Forces, and a little more about how I had spent my time since my discharge, and some more about the things I might do next. Or might not do. I didn't say as much as I might have, but I think she understood more than I put words to. After a while we got off that peg and started talking about things instead, and talked for hours, and then made love after all.

We never did get to sleep. Her plane left at ten and she wouldn't let me take her to it. I didn't argue with her. It was getting very difficult to avoid talking about us and what future we might have. Neither of us had broached the subject, but sooner or later one of us might, and that seemed like a bad idea. I watched her pack. At eight she went downstairs to check out and I went to my room.

From ten, when her plane was supposed to take off, until three, by which time it would have long since arrived, I kept my radio on. I was absolutely certain her plane would crash, and I couldn't decide whether this meant that I was terrified of losing her or that I *wanted* the plane to crash. Then I decided that they were both the same thing, and then I thought that if I had kept my appointment with the psychiatrist it would have been one of the questions I could have asked him. But of course the appointment would have taken place before her flight, and—

I stayed awake all day Sunday, and all that night, and most of Monday as well. I spent most of the time walking around. I ordered a few meals but couldn't get much down. Early Monday afternoon I wrote her a long letter telling her that I loved her and wanted to marry her and adopt her daughter and get a job with a future. I used an entire stack of hotel stationery. Then I panicked because I didn't have her address, and then I remembered that I could get it from the hotel registration card. I decided to do that right away, but first I stretched out on the bed for a moment to think how grand our life would be together, and everything caught up with me and I slept for twenty hours.

I woke up covered with sweat, certain I had mailed the letter. I looked for it on the desk and couldn't find it, and was positive someone on the hotel staff had found it and mailed it for me. I got the housekeeper on the phone and, I'm sure, convinced her only that I was out of my mind. The letter was on the bed. I saw it there and hung up the phone and got a pack of matches and burned every scrap of the letter. I didn't even let myself read it, just burned each sheet and flushed the ashes down the toilet.

I started scanning the yellow pages for psychiatrists, then gave up and threw the book halfway across the room. If I made an appointment I would break it, or forget it. Or lose the address, or miss my train, or something.

Because the obvious truth was that I could not be trusted. I did not know my own mind, and could not, because my mind was in too many places at once. I have seen men freeze in combat, attacked on the right and the left at once and unable to return fire in either direction, standing stupidly in their tracks until bullets knocked them down. I now knew how they felt. I was dangerous, to myself and to anyone near me. I had to be all alone somewhere until things settled down.

Do nothing, I thought.

Two perfect words, answering everything. See Sharon or don't see Sharon? Do nothing. Get a job or don't get a job? Do nothing. Join a mercenary army? Do nothing.

I cashed in all my government bonds, drew all my money out of the several banks who were taking care of it. I bought a money belt at Abercrombie & Fitch and put 193 hundred dollar bills in it, along with my discharge and my birth certificate and my diploma. Then I wore it underneath my clothes and resolved never to take it off, not even in the shower. Wherever I went, I wanted to have everything with me.

Then I packed everything that seemed important into one suitcase and told the bellhop to do what he wanted with the rest. I paid my hotel bill and took a taxi all the way to Idlewild. It would have been cheaper to take the coach from the terminal, but I was sure something would go wrong if I didn't get to the airport as quickly as possible. I got there. All I had decided until then was that I wanted to go someplace warm; it was October, and I didn't want to have to buy winter clothes. By the time I was at the airport I had settled on

Miami, probably because I had been there once, years ago. I was able to get a flight leaving in four hours. I bought a newspaper and spent four hours reading it. I read everything, want ads, stock-market quotations, everything I could find. I was first in line for my flight, first on the plane, first off when we landed.

On the plane I made a list of rules:

DO NOTHING

1. Never write a letter to anyone.
2. Make no phone calls.
3. Don't talk to anyone.
4. No women exc. whores if you have to.
5. Two drinks every day before dinner, otherwise none.
6. Three meals every day.
7. Exercise regularly, swimming and calisthentics, keep in shape.
8. Plenty sleep, sunshine.
9. Don't go anywhere exc. movies.
10. When in doubt, do nothing.

THREE

THE SUN WOKE me. It slanted through my door every morning, a few seconds earlier than the previous day, a few seconds later than the following day. Midwinter had come and gone, and now the sun was rising just a little bit earlier every morning, and so was I. There were no clouds in the sky, hardly a ripple on the surface of the ocean. They could have used my view for an airlines ad. I walked straight from the cabin to the ocean and swam around in it for fifteen or twenty minutes, then came back and built a fire on the beach while I let the sun dry me. I broke the last two eggs into the frying pan and noted that it was my day to row across to Mushroom Key. I ate two eggs every morning and went to Mushroom Key every sixth day to buy a dozen more eggs and whatever else I needed. The store was the closed-in porch of Clinton Mackey's house, and was thus open seven days a week, which saved me the trouble of owning a calendar. I could usually figure out about what day of the week it was and could make a fair stab at the date. This day, for example, was probably a Thursday, because I seemed to remember that it had been Friday when I last rowed over to Mackey's. (Or

27

was that the time before?) And it was somewhere around the middle of January, maybe just past the middle, because the first of the year, as I recalled, had come on a Monday. So if I had had to guess, I would have made it Thursday, January 19. But I didn't have to guess because it didn't matter.

I ate my eggs and sausages, made a cup of instant coffee, drank it, washed my dishes in the ocean, dried them, put them away. I added the empty egg carton to the fire and let it burn itself out. There was a list tacked to the inside of my cabin door, and I read it through, as I did every morning. It was the same list I had made on the plane, the Do Nothing list; I had had to copy it over several times, but I hadn't changed a word, as though the precise phrasing of the original was catechismic in importance.

I read a chapter in my current book while my breakfast got itself digested. It was a paperback, *The Lives of the Great Composers*. This morning I read about Robert Schumann. When he was 34 he developed a profound distaste for high places, for all metal instruments (including keys), and for drugs. He also constantly imagined that he heard the note "A" sounding in his ears. This went on for two years. I learned other things about him, none of which I remembered for very long.

I put *The Lives of the Great Composers* back on top of the portable fridge. It was just as calm and clear outside as before, and warmer. I ran three laps around the island, which was about the size of a football field with the corners rounded. I usually ran six laps, which I figured added up to about a mile, and I usually did push-ups and sit-ups and such, but on rowing days I limited myself to three laps. My island was a good half mile from Mushroom Key, and that much rowing makes up for no end of sit-ups and push-ups and arm-waving.

I sprinted the last hundred yards or so and wasn't even breathing hard when I finished. I cooled off in the ocean, dried off in the sun, and did all the things I had to do before

my trip to the store. My money belt was buried ten yards
behind the cabin. I dug it up, brushed the sand off, fastened it
around me. I put on underwear and a shirt and dungarees and
socks and shoes. I dressed for trips to the store and when the
weather turned cold, which it rarely did; at this rate my few
clothes would last forever. I took a quick inventory, baited a
line with some leftover strips of yesterday's fish, and finally,
with the inside of the frying pan for a mirror, gave my hair
and beard a rough trim. There was no point in shaving and no
place to get a haircut, but I tried to keep myself looking as
little like a wild man as possible. Attracting undue attention
was not consistent with doing nothing.

The boat was small, flat-bottomed, and red. I tossed the
oars into it, dragged it across the sand and into the water.

"Dozen aigs and what-all else?" Clinton Mackey said this
to me once every six days, never altering a syllable. This was
one of the things I liked most about him. There were around
two hundred persons living on Mushroom Key and the sur-
rounding small islands, but it was a rare day when I spoke to
anyone but Clint or his wife or daughter. When a man has
only one conversation a week, it ought to be safe and predict-
able.

"Dozen eggs to start," I said.

"A dozen is twelve, fresh from the hens." He put the
carton on the counter. "I swear you must never get out of the
sun. Must shine at night where you are, sun night and day.
You get any darker, I won't have a choice of serving you or
not. You get any darker, federal government's gone tell me I
got to serve you."

This, too, was an invariable part of our conversation.

"Sausages? Two pounds?"

"Right."

"Oranges?"

"Still have plenty."

"Cooking oil?"

"Got some."

"Cigarettes? Hell no, you don't smoke. 'Less you started since I saw you last?"

"Not yet, Clint."

"Cause the Lord said no," he said. When I had first started coming to the store, Clinton Mackey had tried discussing current events with me. Politics, inflation, the state of the world. I broke him of this by telling him that I was a religious person and didn't believe in radios or newspapers or getting involved with more than one's immediate area. Any mania is instantly excused in the name of religion; he now shut off his own radio the moment he saw me coming.

"Fish line, fish hooks, fish anything?" I shook my head. "Bait? No, you use fish bait, don't you? Catching much lately?"

"Some."

"Whiskey? A quart of shine, which the Lord loves, it being a natural product?" My religion was a devious one. "Not the best I've ever stocked, but better than the last."

Two drinks every day before dinner, otherwise none. "My bottle's running dry," I said. "Better let me have a pint."

"Didn't bring the bottle, did you? Course not, if it's not altogether dry. Do you mind taking a quart? Thing is, I'm out of pint bottles, but I could pour out some soda bottles if you want."

"A quart's all right."

"And bottled water, of course. Three gallons? Four?"

"Three."

"Tins, now, you'll help yourself."

I went over to the shelves of canned goods and picked out what I wanted, then selected a couple of pork chops and a steak from the meat cooler. Clint went down the rest of his list—*String? Twine? Axe handle, whetstone, matches, band-aids, iodine? Coffee? Toothbrush, toothpaste, 'hesive tape? Batteries, dry cell or wet? And what-all else? Dozen aigs and what-all else and what did I forget?*

"Couple new books on the rack," he added. "Might have a look while I pack this up."

There were no books that interested me. I had given up fiction long ago, and the two non-fiction titles on the rack didn't appeal. One was philosophy, which I figured was just fiction without a story line, and the other was a basic guide to atomic physics; I read the first few pages and decided it would be too difficult for me. I still had almost half of *The Lives of the Great Composers* to read, plus a history of Australia and New Zealand.

"Next time the book delivery comes, ask him if he can come up with a paperback dictionary."

"Damn, and he was just here, and you asked me that last week and I forgot. I'll do that, though. I'll remember."

I wasn't quite sure why I wanted the dictionary. It was never that difficult to guess the meanings of those words which I didn't know.

Clint helped me carry the goods to the boat. I was able to dock just a few dozen yards from his store. We made two trips and filled the little rowboat with cartons. "Just about room in there for you," he said, "and you can bet she'll run lower in the water than she did coming over here." This was another of the things that he always said.

"Well, 'bye now."

" 'Bye."

"And I'll remember about that dictionary. Sorry for forgetting, and I'll make a point to remember."

"If you happen to. If not, don't worry about it."

"Man who worries loses his hair." This was a joke—he was bald as a dozen aigs and what-all else. "Take care, now!"

The boat rode lower in the water, which was certainly understandable, but not low enough to make any difference. He went back into his house and I rowed the boat steadily and evenly, putting my back into it, enjoying the way my muscles slipped at once into the proper meter. The sun was high in the sky, the sea was blue and still. It was good to be alive. It was really, honestly good to be alive.

I had reached my little island as the occasional bits of driftwood did, by floating with the tide. Miami was no good at all. People, noise, music, hot outside and frigidly air-conditioned inside. I spent a very bad week there. That week would have been bad anywhere, but Miami made it worse.

Eventually I got to Key West, and that wasn't right either, but it was better than Miami. I compared the two and figured out what it was that made Key West better than Miami, and then it became easy to determine just what sort of place I was looking for.

I got off on the wrong track for a while. I thought it might be ideal to live on a small boat, going wherever I wanted whenever I wanted. I went around pricing boats and decided I had more than enough cash to swing what I wanted.

My list helped me. Buying a boat was spending money, and spending money wasn't doing nothing. Buying a boat also meant owning a boat, and I had already figured out that the less I owned, the better off I was. If I couldn't carry it with me or throw it away, I didn't want it. And worst of all, a boat would enable me to move around. The one thing I wanted to do was stay in one place. Moving around is not doing nothing.

So I let a few real estate men show me rental property on the smaller keys, and one of them took me around Mushroom Key. I was all set to take a small house there when the realtor's motorboat passed a little island the size and shape of a football field, with a little weathered shack at one end of it. I asked what it was, and he said he was damned if he knew, but during the hurricane season it would blow to hell and gone. I asked who owned the island, and if anyone lived in the shack. He said he didn't know. I told him to take me back to Mushroom Key directly. He tried to argue me out of this, and I told him if he didn't do what I said I would throw him overboard and see if he could swim. He thought I was joking, so I threw him overboard. It turned out that he couldn't swim, so I had to jump in and rescue him, but after that he ran me straight back to Mushroom Key without a word.

And it was Clinton Mackey who answered my questions. Who lived in the island? Nobody. A man named Gaines had lived there, a wino, no one ever knew his first name, and several months ago he had disappeared. It was presumed that he had drowned. Who owned the island? Again, nobody. Well, the state, probably, but it didn't really matter who owned it. Gaines sure as hell hadn't owned it, nor paid a cent of rent on it, and he lived there without any trouble, except of course the trouble of drowning.

I started moving in that afternoon. It took me two days to move in with everything I needed, and it took me just about a month to belong there. There was no particular day when it happened. There was just one day after another, exercising and fishing and reading the Do Nothing list, eating and sleeping and taking two drinks of corn whiskey before dinner, swimming and getting brown and rowing to Mushroom Key and back, until somewhere along the way I passed a point without even noticing it.

The point of not returning, I called it.

Because until then I had regarded all of this as a sort of emotional Operation Bootstraps, a self-guided course of therapy with an undefined but never-forgotten goal. Someday, I had thought, I would have it all sorted out, and it would no longer be necessary to stay away from the rest of the world. Some glorious day I would come down from the mountain with two tables of stone in my hands. Some day I would know what role I could best play in life, and I would be ready to play it.

But the island surprised me. It turned unseen from a means to an end. There was no need to leave it, not now, not ever. At the present rate, my money would last forty years. So, it seemed, would I—I had never been in such extraordinarily fine physical shape in my life. My emotional condition was becoming comparably excellent. The bad dreams and the night sweats came further and further apart. Unwelcome thoughts bothered me less and less. I slept well, I ate hungrily, my digestion was sound. Doing Nothing evidently agreed with me. Clinton Mackey provided just the right amount of human contact; I looked forward to seeing him every sixth day, and after half an hour with him I was anxious to get back to my island again.

How easy it was to follow the rules! *Never write a letter to anyone. Make no phone calls*. What could be simpler? *Don't talk to anyone*. I only spoke at Clint's store, and only about business and trivia. *No women exc. whores if you have to*. I thus far hadn't had to. *Two drinks every day before dinner, otherwise none*. The hard part was remembering to take the drinks. Sometimes I forgot them. I never had more than two, and only drank them because it was part of my decalogue. *Three meals every day*. Invariably. *Exercise regularly, swimming and calisthenics, keep in shape. Plenty sleep, sunshine*. No problem there. *Don't go anywhere exc. movies*. The nearest movie was on Key West, and I had no desire to see it. Or anything else. *When in doubt, do nothing*. Five words to live by—but I could have dropped all but the last two. Because I couldn't remember the last time I had been in doubt.

I worked up a good sweat rowing, so as I drew close to my island I put up the oars and uncapped a jug of bottled water and took a long drink. Before I got going again I had a good look at my island—when you row you see where you've been, not where you're going. I reached for the oars, then stopped abruptly and looked over my shoulder again. There was something large and white at the far end of my island, the opposite end from the shack. This was unusual, as most driftwood and flotsam washed ashore at my end. I couldn't make out what it was, and after a few minutes of rowing I stopped and had another look.

It was a boat. And it hadn't washed ashore at all. Someone had steered it there.

Why?

This was a threat, I thought. A very real threat. No one had ever come to my island before. No boat had so much as approached it, let alone landed there.

Until now.

Why?

It could possibly be Gaines, I thought. Maybe the old wino hadn't died, maybe he had gone away somewhere, and had now decided to return and take possession of the shack again. That would be a problem, but not an impossible one. I would have to kill Gaines, of course. Then I would either bury him somewhere on the island or put him back on his boat. Anything buried can be dug up. I would kill him by holding his head underwater, I decided, and then I would put him on his fucking white motorboat and take it a few miles out with my rowboat in tow. Then I would sink his boat with him on it and row back to the island.

Nothing to it, if it was Gaines. But suppose it was someone else?

I tried to imagine who it might be. Clint had guessed that the state owned the island, which seemed possible. If so, they might have sent some nuisance to make sure that I wasn't running a whorehouse or a gambling casino there. Any official attention would be a pain, but I could probably get around it.

If the state didn't own it, the actual owner might be interested in finding out who lived in the shack. He might want to sell me the island, or rent it to me. That was all right. Or he might have decided to build on it, or to sell it to someone else. That was not all right. If it proved to be the case, I had a problem. I could kill this man, whoever he was, but it wouldn't be as simple as killing an old wino. I would have to work it out very carefully.

I resumed rowing. Other possibilities suggested themselves. Someone might have decided to be neighborly, and a few impolite words and phrases would put a stop to that. Or there might be rumors in circulation about the bearded religious fanatic with a store of buried pirate gold. That, I thought, was all I needed. Start killing the ones who showed up and the rumors would only grow. Behave oddly and the rumors would be reinforced. How, then, could I handle that sort of visitor?

This was a threat. Worse, it was an unclear threat.

I was in doubt.

When in doubt—

I breathed deeply, relieved. When in doubt, do nothing. That was the answer. I would do nothing until the doubt cleared, and perhaps the threat would turn out to be no threat at all, and if it was I would worry about it and handle it when the time came.

Meanwhile, what? Stay out on the water? That wasn't doing nothing, that was marking time, wasting time.

I leaned on the oars and pulled toward shore.

There was no one in the boat. I landed at that end of the island so that I could check the boat first off. I did, and it was empty. I beached the rowboat and began walking slowly across the sand. There were footprints leading from the boat along the perimeter of the island toward my shack. The man had evidently walked in the water so that his footprints would disappear, but here and there one remained.

I think Defore was wrong. I think Robinson Crusoe must have torn his hair out when he saw that fucking footprint.

I followed, slowly, carefully, silently. Whoever had come to my island had taken the trouble to try to conceal his footprints. Thus he wanted his presence to be a surprise. And thus he had undoubtedly watched for my appearance in the rowboat and would know I was already on the island. Even so, it seemed sensible to approach him as cautiously and silently as possible.

I studied every tree, every clump of growth. I stopped once to pick up a rock the size of a hen's egg. He might have a gun, or a knife. He might plan to kill me right off.

He was on my island. My island.

I covered sixty yards before I knew where he was. Then I

was able to see the string of footprints cutting across from the shore to the door of my shack.

There were no footprints leading away from the shack. He was in my house.

Obviously I had to kill him. Whoever he was, whatever had brought him here, I had to kill him. He was in my shack. He was on my island, in my shack. Sitting there, the filthy bastard, and waiting for me. In my house, the bastard.

I moved inland so that I could approach the hut from the rear. There were no windows in the hut, but it was possible that he could see me coming through a crack in one of the boards. There were as many cracks as there were boards. I had an advantage, though. The sun was beating down on the back of the shack. It would be at my back and in his eyes. I dropped to the ground, moved forward on hands and knees. The less I showed of myself, the less chance there was that he would be able to see me.

Once I got close I would be able to stop moving, and once I stopped moving he would never see me.

And sooner or later he would show himself. He would know that I was on the island but he wouldn't know where, and sooner or later he would decide to come out and have a look, and then I would have him. He might even wait until dark. Fine. My night vision was always good, and a diet rich in fish coupled with a life without artificial light had made it that much better. Let him wait until dark. Let him sit in the dark, alone and afraid, while I came down on him.

On my island. In my shack—

I stopped, my eyes on the hut, my ears concentrating on every sound. Birds made noise in a tree off to my left. I waited for a long moment, then scampered over to a clump of cover a few yards ahead.

A voice roared, "Hey!"

And, from the shack, something arced high in the air and looped lazily end over end toward me. It landed on the ground not ten yards in front of me and sent sand flying.

A hand grenade.

FOUR

I RAN FORWARD, reached to scoop up the grenade. Even as my hand closed on it I was spinning around to the left, making a full arc and sending the familiar metal egg flying out over the water. I didn't even wait for the explosion but ran ahead full speed toward the shack.

Someone in a dark suit stepped out from the cover of the shack. "Beautiful," he was shouting. "Perfect, Kavanagh."

There was a gun in his hand. If I stopped he would have a clean shot. If I kept going he might freeze, and if he froze I would have him wrapped up before he could kill me. There was no cover for me. All I could do was charge the gun.

"Kavanagh!"

I was fifteen yards from him when the bullet slapped the sand in front of me. I stopped in my tracks.

"Easy, Paul. Easy. Don't come any closer."

"You're on my island."

"Take it easy, Paul."

"My island. My house."

"Relax."

"You threw a grenade at me."

"It was a dud, Paul."

"A grenade."

A smile. "Just a dud, Paul. A dummy, not a real grenade. Had to find out how you'd react. Like poetry in motion. A real grenade would have exploded in the water, Paul. And this one didn't. There was no noise."

I thought. He was right; there had been no explosion.

"You threw a grenade at me," I said. Fifteen yards separated us. He had his gun aimed right at my chest. It looked like a .45, powerful enough so that even a hip or shoulder wound would carry me out of the play.

"Paul—"

"You know my name."

"Why, of course I do, Paul."

"Nobody around here knows my name." I had stopped using my own name when I left Miami. No one on Mushroom Key could possibly have known it. Clint Mackey called me Gordon when he called me anything at all, but I had left it open as to whether that was my first or last name. "Nobody knows my name. You're on my island, you threw a grenade at me. Who the hell are you?"

"You know me, Paul."

I stared at him. Good clothes, light brown hair, tall, thin, eyes hidden behind horn-rimmed sunglasses.

"I don't know you."

"This help?" He took off the sunglasses, squinted at me, replaced them before I could rush him. "How do you stand the sun around here? But I guess you get used to it. And it seems to agree with you, Paul. I'll bet you've never looked better. I preferred you without the beard, personally, but—"

"I don't know you."

"You did once. Calm yourself down, Paul. Take it easy."

"Who are you?"

"We met once. We talked."

"Where?"

"Don't you remember?"

"No."

"I'm really sorry about the grenade. It may have been unnecessary, but I had to know right away whether this back-to-nature routine had turned you hard or soft. You gave me the answer I wanted. I don't think I've ever seen a human being move so fast. You could have stared at the thing trying to figure out what it was and what to do with it, but instead you swung right into action. Beautiful to watch."

"You—"

"Beginning to remember, Paul?"

"Washington," I said.

"That's the boy."

"Washington. Dattner. George Dattner."

I kept my eyes on his face but concentrated on the gun. "How did you find me, Dattner?"

"You were never lost."

"I don't understand."

"You were never out of sight, Paul. Not for very long, anyway. We had a man on you in New York. How did you enjoy Mrs. Jenss, by the way?"

"Who?"

"Sharon Jenss. Our man said she was damned attractive, and you certainly spent a lot of time with her. He said—"

"What the hell is this all about?"

"It's about you, Paul." He smiled. I thought back to our meeting in my room at the Doulton. Dattner seemed different, somehow. Or maybe it was just that I had grown different eyes. "Then you went to Miami, and then a few other places, and then we sort of lost track of you. I knew you were somewhere in the Keys. I didn't know where, but all I had to do was scout around. No matter how careful a man is, he always seems to leave a trail. You used a lot of different names, didn't you, Paul? And did you really throw Mr. Gregg overboard?"

"Who?"

"The real estate man."

"Oh."

"You wouldn't believe the things he said about you. But after I talked with him I knew where you were. So this afternoon I rented a boat and came out here."

"From Mushroom Key?"

"No. Little Table Key. Over that way."

Little Table Key was no farther away from my island than Mushroom Key, but it was almost twice as large. I had been there once and had liked it less than Clint's.

"You haven't been to Mushroom Key?"

"No."

I thought for a moment. "Get back in your boat," I said.

"Huh?"

"Get in your boat and get the hell out."

"Paul, Paul." He shook his head sadly. "Don't you even want to know why I'm here?"

"No."

"Not interested at all?"

"No. You're on my island, you threw a grenade at me. I just want you to go away."

"The Noble Savage," he said. "We need you, Paul."

"We?"

"The Agency."

I looked at him. "You're crazy."

"No. And neither are you, although you sound it right about now. The Agency has a job for you."

"The Agency already sent me away."

"Things have changed."

"Go to hell."

"And you've changed, too, Paul. In plenty of ways."

I didn't say anything. I took a tentative step toward him, but the gun came up and stopped me. He told me not to come any closer.

"You won't shoot."

"One more step and you'll find out the hard way."

"You wouldn't come all the way out here just to shoot me. You want me for something. You don't want to kill me."

"I don't want to get killed by you, either. I'll shoot you in the leg, Paul."

I stayed where I was. "Talk," I said.

"You're ready to listen? You're calm enough?"

"I'm ready."

He drew a breath. "You had me worried for a minute there," he said. "What I've got to say is simple enough. We kept a watch on you because we thought you might come in handy sooner or later. You were going through a bad time emotionally, and we couldn't risk hiring you because the odds were very long against your coming out of it in a form we could use. But men with your qualifications aren't easy to find. So even though we couldn't make any use of you just then, it didn't hurt to tie a string on you."

He paused for no apparent reason. I decided he wanted some sort of assurance that I was listening, so I nodded.

"Then this job came up. When I give you the details you'll see why it's just right for you. Pull it off and there'll be a job open for you."

"I don't want a job."

"You might change your mind. But think of it as an open contract, no strings on either side. You'll be paid for your work on this one, and our rates for free-lancers are more generous than you might think. There's a lot of money in it for you."

"I don't need money."

"Everybody needs money."

"I don't."

"And everybody needs something to do."

"Nothing is plenty."

He grinned. "I read your list," he said. "I like it."

He read my list. He found me, he came to my island, he went into my house, he read my list.

I turned to look across the island. I couldn't see his boat from where I was standing. All I had to do was get him to realize that there was nothing that would make me leave my island. Then he would get back in his boat and head back to Little Table Key and Key West and Washington and never bother me again.

He said, "We need you, Paul."

"That doesn't make sense. How many men work for you? Use one of them."

"We can't use a regular employee."

"Why not?"

"There are reasons, believe me. I'll get to them later."

"You've got hundreds of men under deep cover. Use one of them."

"Can't be done." Smile. "You're the one we need, Paul."

"You had your chance once. The computer said I was no good—"

"Then you weren't. You are now."

"No."

"You really came alive when that pineapple landed at your feet, didn't you? As though you'd been waiting all winter for something to happen. You finally got a chance to use yourself."

"I'm happy here. I like it here."

"Oh, I'll grant that it seems to agree with you. That's a hell of a tan you've got. You can come back here, Paul. Just do what we want and you can take your fee and spend the rest of your life here."

"I can spend it here anyway. Without doing jobs for you."

"Not jobs. Just this one job. And don't be so sure you can."

I looked at him.

"A man named Fenstermacher owns this island. He doesn't even know you're here. Someone could tell him."

I felt muscles tightening in my arms and legs. I made them loosen up again.

"He might make a nuisance of himself, Paul."

"I could work it out."

"Suppose the State Board of Health decided to examine your shack. You'd be surprised how many friends the Agency has and how many people like to do us favors. If you don't turn this trick for us, I've got a hunch you won't be as comfortable here as you have been." His voice softened. "Of course, it works both ways. Cooperation is a two-way street. Play straight with us and you'll never have to worry about Mr. Fenstermacher or the State of Florida. We could smooth things out. Your fee for your work would probably cover the cost of buying the island outright, as far as that goes. And it never hurts to have important friends, Paul. You know that."

He wouldn't get back in his boat and go away forever. I should have known that. He had too much leverage, he was too well placed.

"Just one job," I said, slowly. "Right?"

"If that's the way you want it."

"And then nobody bothers me again."

"If you say so, that's how it'll be. You may change your mind once you're back in action, but the choice is yours all the way, Paul."

The hell it was. If they had a lever now they'd have a lever until hell froze.

I frowned thoughtfully. "How long would it take?"

"As little as one week or as much as three. Split the difference and call it two weeks flat. A fortnight. Two weeks from today you'll be back on your tight little island."

"That's not so bad."

"Not bad at all."

"And I'd have my choice afterward? I could do more work or be left alone forever?"

"Right. No strings either way."

I let my face relax. "You make it sound good."

"It *is* good, Paul."

"I'd like to know what it's all about." I hesitated. "Look, uh, George, I didn't mean to pop off like that. When you go days on end without seeing another human being—"

"I understand completely."

"I mean, no one but me has ever been out here before."

"You don't have to explain, Paul. My apologies."

"Well," I said. I headed for the shack. He was standing just to the right of the doorway. "Suppose I fix us a drink. And you'll want to get out of that jacket. You must be roasting to death in it."

He was shrugging the jacket down over his shoulders just as I drew even with him. His gun hand dropped and the gun pointed at the ground in front of him. I kicked the muscle on the underside of his forearm. He howled and the gun went flying, and he was still howling when the heel of my hand caught the point of his jaw.

He sagged. I grabbed him, one hand bunching his shirtfront, the other between his legs. I hoisted him high into the air and marched across the sand to the water's edge. He was yammering like a little monkey.

I walked straight out into the water until it came almost to my knees. "My island," I was shouting. "My island, my house, my list! My life, you son of a bitch. My life!"

I slammed him down on his back. His legs worked furiously. I stuffed his head underwater and held it there.

"No jobs for you, damn you! My island, my house, my list!"

He couldn't hear me. He was underwater, and he was struggling, and bubbles were coming up through the water from his mouth and nose. After a few moments he went limp, and then, a little later, the bubbles stopped.

FIVE

He Was A lot heavier when I carried him back to shore. His clothes were soaked and his lungs were full of water. It was tempting to leave him there, but I put him over a shoulder and hauled him onto the sand and dropped him face down on it.

I slipped one arm under his stomach, lifted him up a few inches, rolled him back and forth. Half the ocean streamed out of his mouth and nose. I moved in front of him and squatted with a knee on either side of his head and began artificial respiration, pressing down on his lungs, sliding my hands along his arms to his elbows, lifting the elbows, dropping, then going through the whole process again. 1, 2, press the lungs. 3, 4, reach for the elbows. 5, 6, lift the elbows. 7, release.

Mouth-to-mouth resuscitation is supposed to be something like sixty percent more efficient. The thought of applying it to Dattner made me gag. If my method worked, all well and good. If not, tough.

It was bad enough that I had to revive him at all. I couldn't remember wanting anything as much as I had wanted to leave him underwater. He certainly deserved it. He had invaded my privacy and disturbed my life, and murder seemed a minor crime in comparison.

But once rage passed, I saw how inconvenient it would be if he died. He was no Gaines, no friendless wino with no one looking out for him. He was an Agency man on Agency business. There would be men who had known he had come here, and when he didn't return I would have visitors. I could get rid of the boat and the body so that no one would ever be able to prove what had happened to Dattner. But I couldn't keep them off my back. That was the real problem, and Dattner's death would only enlarge it.

Press the lungs, reach for the elbows, lift, drop. I kept working on him, ignoring the increasing suspicion that I was respirating a corpse, and after a while he rumbled and coughed. I stopped. He breathed on his own several times, then quit on me. I started in again and got him going, and this time he stayed with it. He gasped and said something unintelligible, and rolled his head and opened his eyes.

I put my thumbs on either side of his neck and pressed firmly. He blacked out. I checked to make sure that the sudden loss of consciousness didn't interrupt his breathing. There was a momentary lapse but then he came on strong again, nice and regular. I rolled him over onto his back and put my ear to his chest. I had stripped him to his underwear before I started respirating him, and now I realized how white his skin was. Ten minutes of midday sun and he'd be in terrible shape. The sun was on the way down now, so that was no problem.

I listened to his lungs as he breathed. It sounded as though I had gotten almost all of the water out. His pulse was weak but steady.

I went into my shack. At least he hadn't moved anything out of place. I found my roll of twine, cut two lengths, returned to him and tied his ankles together, then put him on his stomach again and tied his wrists together behind his back.

I got undressed. My clothes were wet and I spread them on the beach to dry. It felt good to be out of them, but before I left the shack I put on a pair of swim trunks. That's the trouble with having people near you. You can't feel comfortable naked. I think it's less a matter of inhibition than the equation of exposure with being unprotected. When you're naked, your enemy can get at you.

I found his gun, a .45 automatic. I had no use for it, and I didn't want him to get hold of it, so I threw it halfway to Mushroom Key.

I went back for my rowboat, towed it through the water around the perimeter of my island to where I usually beached it. I carried all of my provisions into the shack and put them away where they belonged. When that was done I waded out to check my fishing line. There were three fishes on it, all the same species, ranging from six to ten inches in length. I didn't know what kind they were but they were the type I usually caught, with flaky meat and a lot of soft tiny bones. I took all three to shore and killed them, although I didn't expect to eat them all. But I had learned not to leave a fish in the water overnight. Something would come and tear it to shreds. This way I would eat what I wanted and use what remained for tomorrow's bait.

Somewhere in the middle of all this Dattner came to again. He made of lot of noise at first, mostly shouting my name. I ignored him. I had discovered before I found my island that people run out of steam if you simply fail to respond to them for long enough. Just because someone says something to you does not mean you are compelled to answer him. It works with strangers, and now it worked with Dattner. Before very long he quieted down and waited for me to notice him.

I let him wait. I chopped the heads and tails off the fishes, slit them down the middle, gutted them and fileted them. I crumpled half a dozen pages of *One, Two, Three* . . .

Infinity, nested them where I built my fires and packed slivers of driftwood over them. When the fire was going nicely I fried two of the fish in cooking oil and ate them both. They were delicious, but then they always are.

"You almost drowned me."

"Not almost. I drowned you, but then I changed my mind and brought you around again. For a while I didn't think you would make it. I almost gave up. I suppose you could say you were dead for a few minutes and then came back to life."

"Jesus Christ."

"You mean the Lazarus bit? I'm honored, but it's not quite the same thing."

"Jesus Christ."

He was on his back, his hands underneath him. I was squatting on my haunches alongside him, finishing a cup of coffee. I had never understood how people could sit on their haunches for long periods of time. I'd always found it painful. When you have all the time in the world to practice, it gets easy.

"One minute you're talking about getting me something to drink, and the next minute my head's underneath the ocean. I never saw anything like it."

"You've been telling me how good I am. Now you know."

"Yeah. Paul?"

"What?"

"Why kill me?"

I finished the coffee, trotted back to the shack to get an orange for dessert. I gnawed at it for a few minutes before answering him. "You came here," I said, finally. "You came here, to my island. I didn't invite you. I didn't want company, you or anybody else. And you wouldn't go away. I told you to go away and you wouldn't go." I shrugged. "On top of that, I got mad. When you're all alone all the time you don't have to keep your temper because nothing makes you lose it. So I was out of practice, and I got mad. Anyway, I couldn't think of a better way to get rid of you.''

"So you tried to drown me."

"I didn't try. I drowned you, and then I changed my mind."

He thought this over while I finished my orange. I set the peel floating in the water. I throw all my organic garbage in the sea where sooner or later something eats it. Cans I burn out and bury. I don't want to make anything dirty.

On the way back I put more wood on the fire. I had a fair stockpile of firewood, and I could always burn planks from his boat.

"Paul?"

"Go ahead."

"Do you have any idea how completely you've changed?"

"Yes."

"I suppose you do. Why did you change your mind?"

"I figured they would miss you and send someone looking for you, so killing you would just complicate things. It would make me feel good for a couple of hours but then it would make my life more difficult."

"No other reason?"

"Like what?"

"Forget it. What happens now?"

"I don't know yet."

"Will you let me go away?"

"As soon as I'm sure you'll leave me alone. I think you probably will, because you must realize I wouldn't be of any use to you. To the Agency. If you don't want me any more, and if you're not set on being vindictive, then there's no reason to keep you here. Or to kill you. So I'll put you in your boat and send you on your way."

"Uh-huh. The funny thing is, I want you more than ever."

"Then you must be crazy."

"Don't bet on it. Look, Paul—"

"Later," I said. I took the frying pan to the water's edge and washed it clean. Usually, on days when I go over to Mushroom Key, I eat a late lunch as soon as I get back and a late dinner a little after sunset. Dattner had fouled up my schedule. The sun was already on its way down, and the two fish filets were lunch. In a few hours I would want to get to sleep, and I hadn't had dinner, and didn't like to eat just before I went to bed. I had planned on having the pork chops.

I would have skipped dinner, but this was no time to abandon my ten rules. They had never been more important. I took two unnecessary drinks from the old pint of corn whiskey. That killed the bottle, and I put it aside to return to Clint next trip. I got the pork chops from the fridge and sauteed them in the frying pan in a half inch of sea water. It's good to cook in and saves adding salt. When the chops were ready I carried the pan over to Dattner. He was on his side, watchimg me.

"You eat a lot."

"One of these is for you, if you want it."

"If I want it. The only thing I want more is a cigarette. I suppose the ones in my jacket are soaked."

"I suppose so."

"There's another pack on the boat."

"It's a dirty habit," I said. "Now's your chance to kick."

His laugh started out ingratiating and wound up honest. He sort of got carried away with it. He asked if I would cut him loose.

"Don't get cute."

"Don't worry."

"Because it wouldn't do you any good. Your gun's in thirty feet of water, and a knife or ax wouldn't give you enough of an edge."

"I've had a lot of training, you know. Unarmed combat."

"That's wonderful."

"You don't sound terrified. I guess I don't blame you. I'll

be a good boy, Paul. Just cut me loose and let me eat and I'll
be good.''

"I undid his ankles first, opening the knot easily. Then I
rolled him over and worked on the length of twine around his
wrists. It had gotten wet, and I had a tough time picking it
apart.

"Why not cut it?"

"I don't want to ruin the twine."

"You're putting me on."

"No."

"Well, I'll be a son of a bitch," he said. "And this is the
joker who has all the money he needs. What is that, a tenth of
a cent's worth of twine? You don't need money, but you'll
spend all day working on a knot and—"

I opened the knot. He turned over, sat up, rubbed his
wrists.

He said, "A couple of feet of twine—"

I handed him a pork chop and told him to shut up and eat it.
I ate mine. When he was done I threw the bones into the
water. I opened the quart bottle of shine and brought him two
ounces in an empty tin can.

"Aren't you drinking?"

"No."

"I forgot. Two a day before dinner and no more, right?"

"One of the things we won't talk about is the list."

"Don't get angry—"

"I'm just telling you."

"Sure." He drained the can in two swallows. "Smooth,"
he said.

"Homemade corn."

"Nothing like it. They make it around here?"

"I don't know."

He asked if he could go to the boat for cigarettes. I told him
no—he might have a gun there, or might try to get away. He
said he would give me his word. I just looked at him. He
asked, then, if *I* would go for his cigarettes. I told him not to

be silly. He stopped talking.

I said, "About the twine. You don't understand anything at all. The cost of it doesn't matter. It's the inconvenience. The greatest nuisance in the world is garbage. I don't throw things into the water unless they get eaten sooner or later. So—"

"What about the bones?"

"They'll break down. Fish will eat parts of them and pick at the meat and marrow, and the rest will nourish some form of life. And—"

"And my gun?"

"Lesser of two evils. I don't usually throw guns in the sea. I don't usually have to. Shut up, will you?" He did. "So with twine, little unusable bits of twine, I have to burn them. That's easy enough, but it's something else that has to be done. And twine doesn't burn that well. They treat the fibers with some sort of crud and it stinks when it burns.

"And if I waste twine, sooner or later I'll have to buy more twine. Which means remembering to pick it up at the store, and carrying it to the boat, and having it take up so much space in the boat, and carrying it ashore and putting it away again. The less often I have to do this, not just with twine but with everything else—"

"I get the point."

"Do you? I don't mean the twine, I mean the real point. That there's a reason for everything I do. That I have worlds of time out here with nobody in my way. That I've gradually worked things out so that my life runs exactly the way I want it to. Whenever I find that I've got something in the shack that's useless, I get rid of it. I use books I'm finished with to start fires. I used to have a fork and a spoon, small ones for eating, and one day I realized that I was eating all my meals with my fingers anyway, or else eating with the cooking fork. So I dug a hole and buried the tableware. I don't want anything extra around. I don't want anything to get in my way."

"It's an unusual attitude."

"It works for me."

"Uh-huh."

I left to take a leak, and that reminded him that he had a similar function to perform. I told him where to go, and to kick sand over it when he was done. On the way back he said, "Paul? There's something you might want to hear, but it refers to something you said not to mention."

"Huh?"

"It refers to, uh, the list."

"Oh, go ahead."

He chose his words carefully. "One item there, one of the maxims, was about not talking to anyone. Unnecessarily, that is."

"So?"

"Well, if you think back over the past few minutes. When you started explaining about the twine, and your views on garbage, uh, and getting rid of useless articles. You didn't have to bother explaining all of that to me. That was what I suppose would come under the heading of unnecessary talk. Until then you hardly talked at all, but now it's as if you want to talk, to have a conversation."

I didn't say anything.

"I'm not making any point. I just thought it was something you might like to hear about."

I didn't answer him, and he let it lie there. After a while I said that it was getting dark and suggested we move closer to the fire. We did. I asked him if he wanted coffee.

"If you're having some," he said.

I poured fresh water into my cast-iron kettle and put it on the fire. When it boiled I added powdered coffee, stirred it, scooped out two cans and gave him one.

"Thanks." he said.

"I don't have sugar or cream."

"This is fine."

"If you want to get those cigarettes out of your jacket, you can probably dry them out."

"And they'll be smokable?"

"If they don't rip, and if you don't scorch them."

He got the pack and opened it. There were seven cigarettes, and two had already come apart. I spread out four alongside of the fire. The last one I kept. I found a piece of firewood that was just burning at one end, and I fished it out and toasted the cigarette with it. The paper got brown in spots but stayed intact. I gave it to Dattner and held the flame while he lit up.

I asked him if it was all right, and he said he couldn't remember one ever tasting better.

I sat back and watched the fire and drank my coffee. I thought suddenly of the paperback dictionary and the possible reasons why I might want one. A dictionary is a book full of words. Words are talk, talk is communicating is other people.

If Dattner hadn't told me that I was breaking one of my rules, I would have gone on to tell him that my major preoccupation was with water. I went through three to four gallons of bottled water a week. I needed it for drinking, for washing, for cooking, for coffee. If there was only a way to have a fresh-water source on the island—

Don't talk to anyone.

And that had been such an easy rule, and for such a long time. Something I might like to hear about, he had said. Something I might like to think about, he had meant. Something he might like me to think about.

He said, "Maybe I could use the fire to dry my clothes."

"It doesn't work. The sun will dry them in the morning."

"I'm staying overnight, then?"

"Did you have other plans?"

He laughed. I thought he was going to say something, but he didn't. He finished his cigarette and was going to flick the butt away. Then he remembered and put it in the fire. That pleased me.

I said, "Okay."

He looked at me.

"Let's hear about the operation."

"The what?"

"The Agency thing, the job," I said patiently. "The reason you're here. Don't look surprised. You finally found the right bait, you shouldn't pretend to be shocked that there's a fish on the line. You're trying not to smile. Go ahead and smile. And then tell me all about it."

SIX

"PICTURE AN ARMS shipment," Dattner was saying. "All U.S. government-issued goods, nothing but the best. The government wants to send them to friends. Instead the bad guys get them."

"So?"

"So the idea is to get them back."

I looked at him. "That's all?"

"No, of course not, Paul. I just—"

"Because it doesn't make any sense. It happens all the time. If I had a dime for every American in Vietnam shot with a U.S.-made gun . . . a dime, hell, if I had a grain of sand for every one I'd have a beach. It happens everywhere, all over the world. We send guns to guerrillas and the government forces confiscate them. We supply government troops and the guerrillas steal them. Most of the time it's a case of a government official going bad and turning a fast dollar. Other times the weapons are taken in military action."

"And we never try to recover them?"

"If we do, I never heard about it."

"We make a stab at it once in a while, Paul. Mostly we try

to buy them back, and you'd be surprised how often it works. But as a general rule you're absolutely right. Shipments get derailed and it's part of the game, and we have plenty of factories turning out plenty of guns, and it's easier to make new guns than chase the old ones. By the time the enemy gets them, they're generally obsolete, anyway."

"So?"

"So this is different."

He picked up a cigarette and made a production of lighting it. He was waiting for me to ask him how it was different. Then he could tell me that was a good question, and I could say—

What I said was, "Just tell it straight. There are no points given for suspense and dramatic effects. Just tell it."

"The direct aproach, eh? But sometimes a straight line isn't the shortest distance between two points. Sometimes a great circle route—"

"Not here. Not on my island."

A smile, a nod. "Okay. To hell with drama. This isn't ordinary weaponry, conventional stuff. We're talking about a shipment that's worth in excess of two million dollars and fits into four trucks. We're talking about the most highly sophisticated combat devices ever produced for guerrilla warfare. I don't have to tell you about guerrilla warfare. You had ten years of it. All I have to say is that this gear makes the stuff you used in Asia look like water pistols. They didn't give you fellows toys like this. They've been making them all along, but they were never okayed for combat use. Not because they don't work. The testing reports would knock you out. But because nobody would buy escalation on that scale.

"Like atomic grenades, for example. One man throws one and clears three acres. Like nuclear mortars. Gas grendades. Do you realize what you've got when you can combine the knockout power of a nuclear blast with the maneuverability of a mortar? Do you realize how effective they'd be against guerrillas? Or how well they'd work *for* guerrillas?"

"The real dirty stuff."

"Right."

"We kept hearing rumors that we were getting stuff like that. Or that the other side was." I remembered a tangle we had in Laos on a patrol deep in Pathet Lao territory. I tried to imagine what it would have been like if we'd had that kind of weaponry.

Or if they had it.

"I could go on, Paul, but you wanted it engraved on the head of a pin. It's choice stuff, the real dirty stuff. The decision to give it to some friends was ultra-top level. It didn't make the papers. It never will—if the question ever comes up, we'll deny we ever had it, we'll insist they made it out of old tire tubes in Burma, we'll lie our heads off no matter who says what. Hell, giving the stuff out couldn't get fifty votes in the House or twenty in the Senate."

"Keep talking."

"I was just noticing the stars. It's beautiful out here, isn't it?"

"Yes."

"Peaceful. I could see how a man could enjoy spending nights here, under the stars, sitting beside a fire—"

"You made your point, Dattner."

"George."

"You made your point. Get on with it."

He flicked ashes from his cigarette. "You can figure out the rest, can't you? The shipment was dispatched—not, needless to say, through the usual channels. You can also guess who was supposed to receive it."

"The hell I can. I haven't looked at a newspaper or heard a radio in months. For all I know we sent the crud to Canada."

"I forget how out of touch you've been."

"Not out of touch. Call it—no, forget it, forget word games. Where were they supposed to go?"

"To guerrillas, and in this hemisphere, and now you can guess, Paul, because it's the same guess you would have made a year ago. You with me?" I was. "But instead of going where they were supposed to go, a wheel came off and they wound up in the wrong hands. At first it looked as though they were going to go to the bad-guy government that our good-guy guerrillas were trying to overthrow, and that would have been more or less terrible, but it turned out that it was worse than that. A lot worse, because we could have made a good stab at blocking that shipment.''

He put his cigarette in the fire. ''Instead it turns out that the new destination of all this hell on wheels is yet another group of guerrillas, but in this instance they're bad-guy guerrillas who'll use them to knock hell out of a good-guy government. Four truckloads of this garbage is just about enough to do it, too, but it hardly matters whether they win or lose, because the U.S.A. loses either way. If they make it, we've lost the cornerstone of free Latin America. If they flop, a lot of people will want to know what happened. It won't even help us to deny that these were our goods, not even if anybody's fool enough to believe us. Because then people will ask how the hell we managed to let the enemy smuggle dynamite like this into the western hemisphere. Did I say dynamite?'' He snorted. ''It's about time we changed our lingo. Dynamite is something kids use to celebrate the Fourth of July. Where was I?''

''If we lose we lose, and if we win we lose.''

''That says it. There's only one way to come out of this clean. We have to get the shipment back before delivery is made.''

''Or prevent delivery.''

''Isn't that the same thing?''

''Not really. If the object is to prevent delivery, all you have to do is destroy it. If it's in trucks you drop bombs on them. If it's on a ship you sink it. If it's in a plane you shoot it down. It sounds like a job in the Air Force, doesn't it?''

He grinned. ''This stuff is nuclear, remember? You blow it up and you have fallout.''

''So you say *Sorry about that* and explain that it won't happen until next time.''

"Even if it's in a friendly country?"

"Even if it's in London."

"And suppose it's in the United States. Then what?"
I stared at him.

"Because that's where it's at, Paul. It's in the midwest right now, smack in the Heartland of America, as the fellow says. We know the location and we know the players on the other team. We know how they're going to ship it. We can even make a hell of a good guess when they're going to ship it. It'll go by air, of course, and takeoff time will be in more than a week and less than three."

"If it's in the States, and you can pinpoint the location—"

"Let me go on, Paul." He lit another cigarette, but without theatrics this time. "We could bomb the storage site, of course."

"That's not what I was going to say."

"I know, but it's one of the things we've thought about. Our computers estimate it would cost us two-thirds of the population of three counties, plus long-term fallout victims scattered over four states. That's been tentatively ruled out."

"That's nice."

"Uh-huh. There are other things we can try. We can let them load the plane and then knock it out of the skies. The plane will be a jet. We know this, too, because the plane is already in this country. We know everything about the plane because they stole it from us. Don't interrupt me. We know everything, that is, except where they're keeping it. But we'll probably spot it when it takes off, and we can probably keep interceptors on its tail. But they're not idiots on the other team, Paul. They won't cooperate by flying over water. They'll stay over land, and we'll have to try for an intercept over relatively unpopulated South American terrain. We asked the computer to estimate chances of a successful intercept and guess the probably casualties. It blew three transistors. We'll try for that intercept if push comes to shove, but we look on it as a last line of defense."

"Go on." My head was aching for the first time in months. I wasn't used to hearing people talk. "Go on," I said. "Now explain why you can't throw a battalion of marines and paras around the place."

"We could."

"Of course you could."

"And they'd take all our pretty toys and use them on us."

"They wouldn't have the manpower to hold out."

"Right. We'd win. But they'd probably last as long as they could, and it would be expensive for us. We might try it anyway. More likely, we'd try to use para divisions to cut them off when they try loading the plane. Again, it's something that would probably work, unless there was a foulup somewhere along the line. Which might happen."

"If they already stole the weapons and a good-sized cargo jet, I'd say foulups have a tendency to happen."

"You're not the first person to notice that." He chuckled. "Paul, let me save time. You're not going to think of a line of defense that either a man or a machine hasn't already suggested. Some have been ruled out and some are in the planning stage. None is ideal. An ideal operation would recover the weapons intact with no loss of life on our side and no publicity. If it doesn't work, then the other procedures come into play one by one. What we want you for is the first step, the ideal play."

"Which is?"

"They stole 'em from us, and now we steal 'em back again."

"Who is we?"

"Two men. You and me." He watched my eyes. "No clever answer?"

"No."

"You on the inside, an unknown. We know they must have men in our camp but no one will know about you. You on the inside and me on the outside. You don't know the physical plant, you can't visualize it, but you can take my word it's feasible. It can be done."

"I'll take your word."

"No immediate doubts, No great show of surprise?"

"None." I stood up. "I saw it coming."

He looked worried.

"I made a mistake," I told him. "I should have drowned you before. All I had to do was do nothing, leave you there in the water. I could have used you for fishbait and your boat for firewood and no one would ever have come looking for you. No, don't get up. Don't even try, or I'll knock you down again. They don't know you're here. They lost interest in me the day I checked out of the Doulton. You're all on your own."

"Paul—"

"Shut up. This isn't an Agency job, it's your job. All yours. The last time I saw you, the only other time I saw you, you told me my trouble was that I learned how to think. Don't forget it. You told me I wouldn't take a black pill. I won't take one with a sugar coating either. You want me for something, then you give it to me straight and I say yes or no."

He started to get up. I let him get most of the way, then kicked his feet out from under him.

I said, "There are two things you can do. You can stick to your lie or find a new one, and if you do I'll know it, and I'll take you out and drown you. Or you can start over without the frills and do it right. It's your move."

"You would drown me."

"You already knew that."

"We had a meal together, we talked, and you would drown me."

"Oh, cut the shit."

"You're a beauty. They never should have let you get away. I knew it the day I talked to you, I saw things that wouldn't fit on their graphs. I knew you'd crack and I knew you'd mend, and—"

"Leave me out. Let's hear it."

"Sure," he said. "You may not like it, but this time it's straight. And it's a honey."

● ● ●

It wasn't bad. Everything was about as he had described it, he explained, except that the United States government wasn't in on it. Both the military and the civilian intelligence people had it on very good authority that the whole shipment had already arrived in South America, and the Agency was busy rushing men to that area to try to minimize the damage.

"But it isn't there, Paul. It's still in the States. I know it, and I have to be the only person who does. Nobody came and told me. There was data coming across my desk, miscellaneous bits and pieces that didn't add up to anything concrete. You could feed the whole mess to a computer and not even find out what time it was."

But he sensed something, enough to make it worth his while to take a quiet little trip west. He nosed around and found out he was right. He already had me traced as far as Florida. A private investigator placed me in Key West, and he did the rest of the detecting himself.

"You rememer that conversation we had? I was talking to myself as much as to you. I could put this package on the right desk and come out neck deep in glory. I don't want glory any more. I'd rather be up to my neck in money."

He figured a half share would come to a million dollars. A half share was all he wanted. With that kind of money around, all of it tax-free, it made no sense to haggle over a split. A million dollars was a footnote in an administrative budget. It was also his present take-home pay for the next eighty-seven years and seven months. And it was one half of what he was certain he could get from a well-heeled refugee group in Tampa.

"They're in the same camp as the good guys who were originally set to receive the stuff. That's the real beauty of it, Paul. They're on the same side. The goods go to their original destination, the U.S. comes out clean, our friends down south avoid getting themselves atomized, and you and I cut up a two-million-dollar pie."

There were more details, fine points. I let him finish. Then he asked me what I thought, and I said I wanted to think it over, and he told me that was just the answer he hoped I'd give him. He finished his last cigarette, and I walked him down to the boat to get his other pack. He opened it and flipped the strip of cellophane away. I didn't say anything about it. He lit up and asked me if I didn't feel chilly. I said I didn't, that I rarely noticed temperature changes. He said he wished his clothes were dry. I waited until he had finished his cigarette and flipped it into the water. It was amazing how quickly he forgot to behave.

"Beautiful out here," he said. "Really beautiful."

"It is," I said.

Then I spun him around and stabbed three fingers into his gut two inches south of his navel. I pulled it enough so that nothing would get ruptured. He doubled up in agony but couldn't make a sound. That's one of the nice things about that particular jab.

The next thing he knew he was on his back in two feet of water, just about halfway between the top and the bottom.

I kept him under for maybe ten seconds. His eyes were open, but it was impossible to catch his expression in that light, not with the water in the way.

I pulled him up and let him sputter and breathe. I didn't say anything, and he couldn't. Then I stuck him under again.

Ten more seconds and I brought him up. I had never before seen such terror on a human face. I wasn't doing anything to him, he wasn't even swallowing any water, but that hardly mattered. He was in very bad shape.

"You're about to go down for the third time," I told him gently. "The third time is the charm. You seem to think that you have to tell me what I want to hear, but all I want to hear is the truth. Forget about persuading me. Concentrate on staying alive."

He didn't say a word. His mouth moved but that was all.

"You've got ten seconds, George." If he wanted me to call him George this was a good time to start. "It shouldn't take you more than three sentences. When your time's up you go under, so you'd better finish before I get bored."

The words came out of him in one uninflected stream, no punctuation anywhere. But it only added up to two sentences.

"The government still has the stuff in a warehouse. It won't be shipped but we can steal it and split two million cash."

SEVEN

THE FOLLOWING MONDAY I wore work clothes into a barber shop in Orlando. I was cleanshaven but shaggy. I walked out with a crewcut. I took a bus to Jacksonville, and in the men's room of the Greyhound station I changed to a suit and covered the crew cut with a wig. In Jacksonville I rented a Plymouth from a national car-rental agency, using a Florida driver's license made out to Leonard Byron Phelps. I drove the car to Atlanta and destroyed the license as soon as I had turned in the car.

I flew to New Orleans, where I disposed of the wig. I used three different airlines and as many names to reach Minneapolis. I slept on planes and dozed in terminals, but didn't stop at any hotels en route. In Minneapolis there was a foot of snow on the ground and a raw wind that never quit. I had three double whiskeys at a downtown bar and spent sixteen hours at a Turkish bath. I did a little sweating and a lot of sleeping, but I made sure I fitted in a massage and alcohol rub. The rubdown made my suntan a little less pronounced.

The tan was the one thing that bothered me. It would have made me conspicuous anywhere, but in that part of the country at that time of year it drew stares from everyone. I had a cover to explain it—that wasn't the problem. It was just that I wanted to avoid being memorable. My shape and size are ordinary enough, my face is forgettable, and the tan was the only thing that got in the way.

I had tried a skin bleach earlier. I bought it in a Negro neighborhood in Atlanta. It was a sale the clerk may never forget. I tried it out in a lavatory, testing it on a portion of my anatomy which I rarely expose to the public. The effect was blotchy and unnatural. I suppose repeated applications might have had the desired effect, but it didn't seem worth the risk.

I took a bus to Aberdeen, South Dakota, a town with twenty thousand people and one car-rental agency. They gave me a two-door-Chevy with heavy-duty snow tires, and the clerk said he guessed there wasn't much snow where I came from. I showed him a driver's license that swore I was John NMI Walker, from Alexandria, Va.

I had not known there was so much snow in the world. It came down all the way to Sprayhorn, a fifty-three mile drive that took me almost three hours. The windshield wipers couldn't keep up with it. I found the motel, the only one in the little town. They had a room for me, but the girl on the desk said they hadn't expected me until the following day.

I told her the office must have made a mistake. It was my mistake, I was early, and the reservation telegram that Dattner had sent from Washington had been according to plan.

The room was better than I had expected. Wall-to-wall carpeting, a big double bed, and three thousand cubic feet of warm air. I unpacked my suitcase. The closet got two dark suits with Washington labels and the uniform of a major in the United States Army. The dresser got most of the rest.

I had two sets of identification. My wallet was crammed with the paraphernalia of John NMI Walker, everything from credit cards (Shell, Diner's, Carte Blanche) to army stuff. Only the government papers suggested that J. NMI W. was a military type. They gave my rank as major, all except one dated three years ago which had me down as captain. The new rank had been inserted in ink, with initials after it.

Every shred of Walker ID was counterfeit. It was all high quality, but there wasn't anything there that an expert couldn't spot as phony.

My other new self, Richard John Lynch, substituted quality for volume. Mr. Lynch had no credit cards, no driver's license, no auto registration, no checkbook stubs. Mr. Lynch didn't even have a wallet. All he had was a flat leather pass case that held a simple little card with his name, picture, fingerprints and description. The name was his and the rest were mine.

Mr. Lynch's identification announced only that he was an accredited agent of that very intelligence Agency which employed George Dattner and which had decided against employing me. And Mr. Lynch's ID was the genuine article, absolutely authentic in every respect. There was only one way on earth that anyone could possibly discredit Mr. Lynch's ID, and that was by pointing out that no one with his name, face, or fingerprints had ever worked for the Agency in question.

I had dinner down the road, then drove back to the motel. I was gone a full hour, but no one tossed my room during that time. I checked rug fibers and powder flecks, and everything was as I'd left it, and nobody is that good. I stretched out on the bed. Twenty minutes later there was a knock on my door. I asked who was there, and a voice called, ''That you, Ed?'' I said he had the wrong room, and he excused himself and went away.

They were certainly slow, but after all I hadn't been expected until the following day. I prowled around the room looking for bugs. I didn't find any, but couldn't swear there were none. According to George, any tap operation involving someone who was presumably hip included more than one device. There were always one or two obvious mikes for the subject to locate and one or more subtle ones for him to miss. My room at the Doulton, for example, had had a very clever lamp on the bedside table, along with the more notice-able gimmick in the ceiling fixture.

Unless military intelligence hadn't picked up this proce-dure, and he thought they had, then the absence of readily identifiable listening devices meant a room was clean. It didn't matter. I would treat the room as bugged regardless.

I watched television for two hours without paying attention to it. There was one channel and the reception was terrible. I listened to the news on the chance that it would have some-thing important to tell me. It didn't, and I went to sleep when it was over.

I was up well ahead of the sun. I showered and shaved and put on Maj. Walker's uniform. The fit was good enough to be true and not too good for a cover identity. They tossed the room while I had breakfast, and I would have known it without the rug fibers or powder. They put a pair of socks back on the wrong side of the drawer. That was good enough to mention to George, if I ever saw him again.

At eleven o'clock I got in the car. I was supposed to have arrived that morning around ten, and my orders called for me to report to my new commanding officer immediately upon arrival. That was fine, I was back on schedule. I drove through the center of Sprayhorn and northwest toward the base. I had my wallet in my hip pocket, my orders on the seat beside me, and my Agency card in the inside breast pocket of my jacket. I drove six miles. The snow had stopped during the night, but there was enough of it on the road to make the drive an ordeal. I had to concentrate on it when I would have preferred to spend the time reminding myself who I was. I was an Agency man pretending to be a career officer. George insisted it was much easier that way, that double covers reinforced each other. I wasn't so sure.

The compound would have been hard to miss. It was the only thing on the road besides snow. A fifteen-foot fence, barbed and electrified, circled it. Rectangled it, if you prefer. Inside there was a lot of empty ground and three concrete block buildings. They were all about the same size, and they were all about forty-five feet tall, and none of them had any windows. There were also soldiers all over the place, all in heavy brown overcoats, none performing any apparent function.

A sign reappeared every fifty yards along the fence. It announced that all of this was the product testing division of the General Acrotechnic Geodetic Corporation, that admittance was restricted to authorized personnel, and that the fence was electrified. The last statement was true, the middle one misleading, the first a lie. There was no such thing as the General Acrotechnic Geodetic Corporation and probably never would be, since the phrase was gobbledygook. Admittance was restricted specifically to military personnel specifically assigned to the base, the correct name of which was Fort Joshua Tree. It was named for a longdead general who would have been sickened by the things inside the place, a far cry from muskets and cavalry sabers. New times, new customs.

There was a corporal at the front gate. We played the salute game and I gave him my orders. He told me where to park and which building to enter. I parked where he said, received and returned salutes, and showed my orders to another corporal in the entrance hall of the appointed building. This kept happening until I reached the offices of General Baldwin Winden. His secretary announced me over an intercom. He said he wasn't expecting me, and the secretary said something about misdirected memos and took my orders inside. I opened the intercom and listened to them discuss me. My tan was mentioned, damn it. The general and his secretary tried to figure out who or what I was and decided that asking me might save time.

"I don't know what he's doing here," I heard the general say, "but if it says he belongs here, that's all that counts."

The military mind. Nothing ever changes, orders are always orders. Extraordinary.

I went into the general's office. We saluted each other, and I made a point of doing nothing until the secretary went away.

I figured he would listen in on the intercom, but that was fine with me. When the door closed I said, "General Baldwin, I—"

"Winden," he said. "Baldwin's my first name, Major."

It wasn't a slip on my part. It was the sort of bad prep military men liked to expect from civilian agencies.

"Hell," I said. "They never get anything right." I put a finger to my lips, moved it to my ear, then pointed at the walls and ceiling. He looked at me as though I was bucking for a Section Eight. I handed him my Agency ID. He flipped it open and did a take that was almost too good to be true. You could almost see a cartoon-style light bulb over his head.

"Well, well, well," he said. "Have a seat, Mr. Lynch. You know, I'm not surprised. Something about those orders didn't ring true." Oh, sure. "Sit down, tell me what I can do for you. Oh, we can talk here, sir. Oh, don't you worry now, we can talk here, sir. This is United States Army property, there hasn't been a civilian on the grounds since the fence went up. Except for your sort of people, of course. Sit, sit . . ."

I sat. I had wondered what sort of general they would pick to run a candyass warehouse in the middle of South Dakota, and now I knew, and he was better than anything I could have dreamed up.

"So you came to see us," he said. "Well, well, what can I do for you people? Hmmm?"

"You can find me something innocuous to do for the next three weeks," I said. "If there's an empty office, put me in it and pile papers on my desk. If anybody asks, I'm Major John Walker and I'm doing something confidential. Don't tell anyone otherwise, not even your secretary. And don't—"

"Now one moment, sir! Now one moment!"

I stared at him.

"You have no authority here, sir. None! You are a civilian, sir, and you have no lawful right to be here, let alone furnish me with instructions. No right at all! You are a civilian and we are military and—"

I stood up, and he stopped talking. Just like that. I wondered if General Tree was as much of a washout as this moron.

I broke the silence. I said, "If you want to order me out, for Christ's sake go ahead. I left the middle of a Brazilian summer for this. They put me up here in Eskimoland and issued me a pretty little soldier suit and forgot to put an overcoat in my bag. I'm supposed to spend three fucking weeks doing nothing waiting for something that isn't going to happen. I couldn't sleep last night and I had a stinking breakfast this morning and the clowns who searched my room this morning did everything but autograph my pillow. You can't want me out of here as much as I want to get out of here, sir, and I'm sure this is God's own country in the summer, but—"

"Sir!"

I stared at him, and this time he gave me his guarded look. "You'll be here for three weeks?"

"I'll be here until your shipment goes out, which could be any time during the next three weeks but which we both know will be on the fourth of February."

"The date has not yet been determined, Mr., uh, Lynch."

"Maybe they haven't notified you." And, as an afterthought, "Or maybe our information is wrong."

"The latter, I'm sure. The date will purposely remain undetermined until the last moment." If he honestly believed they wouldn't set the date until they were ready to give him the word, then he was too dumb to live. "Now let me see, Lynch. You're concerned with the shipment?"

I just nodded. I had already been enough of a wiseass.

"But you're civilian. We should have someone from Military Intelligence."

"You probably do."

"If that were so, I would know about it." The hell he would. I told him his boys would probably have a man or a team down any day but that I was under orders to work independently.

"We have an interest in this ourselves," I said. "You know the eventual destination of the shipment."

He named a military compound in Florida, another in Texas, a third in the northeast, a fourth in California. It was the most obvious breach of security since the Trojan horse. I had trouble repressing a fairly sincere moment of civic outrage.

Instead, I filed the information. George had thought everything was being routed to Florida, and either he or the general was wrong. I figured anybody would have to pick the general for this honor, but George might have misread something. Four trucks, four destinations—there was a certain degree of logic there.

I said, "I mean final destinations." He looked completely blank. This was a whole new concept to him. "Without going into detail," I said, "The goods will be shipped onward from the places you mentioned. That's where we come in, that's where it stops being military and turns civilian."

"Oh, I see."

"So while the first delivery stage is legally your baby, my team wants me here. I think it's about as necessary as it is warm, but orders are orders." There was a phrase he could cuddle up with. "So I have to be here unless you order me out. I'll try not to get in anyone's way, believe me. Keep me a secret. A blown cover would look bad. I went five years in the Amazon without getting blown, and I ought to be able to do three weeks in South Dakota."

He stood up, and I saluted. He had trouble returning it; I could see it didn't seem right to him. You didn't spend your life getting to be a general just to salute camouflaged civilians.

"I will give you whatever help I can," he said, stiffly.

"I'll appreciate it. I'm bunked down at the motel, and I'm under orders to go on living there. I'm frankly damned if I know why."

"Orders," he said.

"I doubt that anyone will ask, but my story will be that I'm awaiting assignment of permanent quarters. I don't think the point will come up—"

"I doubt it, sir."

"—but just in case. Well. Do you have an office available? It will have to be private, but that's my only requirement. And could I figure on moving in around two this afternoon? Good, very good."

I extended my hand, and we shook. I could tell he liked it a hell of a lot better than a salute.

EIGHT

THAT AFTERNOON THEY had an office ready for me, and, more important, a heavy overcoat. A few junior officers managed to walk past my open door and take a quick glance inside. This might be simple curiosity—what else could they do for kicks?—or the word might already have gotten around that I was an Agency snoop. It didn't matter. The on-base intelligence crew was no threat, and if MI was going to send in a team, that was something to worry about later. The possibility always existed that the Agency had an undercover op already planted. George was certain this wasn't so, but that I didn't have to worry anyway. My Brazil cover would help explain the fact that he didn't know me, or I him.

The only problem with the Brazil background was that I couldn't speak Portuguese. I had a touch of Spanish, though, and my accent was poor, and if anyone started talking to me in Portuguese I could try answering in the worst Spanish possible. "Never could keep from mixing up Portugee and the old Español, and where I was they were all Indians and we talked the native jive"—and then hit 'em with a mixture of Cambode hill dialect and gibberish.

I left the office around four. From Sprayhorn I sent a wire to T.J. Morrison at a hotel in downtown Washington. It was an hour later there, so George would be picking up the wire in an hour or less. He was supposed to have checked in at the hotel around noon, signing in but not going to his room. Now he would pick up the telegram, and then he would never come back.

I wired: BIRTHDAY GREETINGS AND ALL OUR LOVE. WISH WE COULD BE WITH YOU. KEN AND SARAH. It didn't mean anything. Any message from me meant only that I was on the spot and everything was going according to plan. The important thing was maintaining contact without leaving any threads dangling that could possibly tie Walker-Lynch to George Dattner. He could communicate with me in any of a dozen ways, because it was to be expected that I would get messages from Washington, but we needed elaborate arrangements for me to reach him.

That night I hit a few bars until I found one with a colonel's wife who was looking to get picked up. She was crowding forty and overly fleshed. She was drinking gin and coke. "A traditional drink down home," she drawled. "If y'all spent any time in Nawlins, Ah wouldn't have to tell y'all that."

I had spent enough time in New Orleans to know that y'all is plural, so either the accent was artificial or she was seeing two of me. Or both. She was half in the bag when I got there and I kept her company through three more gin and cokes and they hit her pretty hard, tradition or no.

On the ride back to my room she unzipped my fly and told me how her husband was a bastard bird colonel who only got stationed where it was cold enough to freeze her blood. And by Gawd a girl had to do something to keep warm, didn't she? Then she started giggling.

In bed she behaved wildly, out of passion or practice, and seemed to enjoy herself. God knows why. Afterward she lay back with her head on my pillow and a cigarette in her mouth. When her eyes closed I took the cigarette from her mouth and carried it into the bathroom and flushed it away. I came back and sat down next to her and watched her. Her mouth had fallen open and she was breathing noisily through it.

I studied her. Her hair needed reblonding. A full half inch of brown root showed. I touched her hair. It remained unruffled, artfully sprayed into place, and it felt like plastic.

Old acne scars showed dimly beneath her facial makeup. The rest of her skin was a washed-out white. I touched parts of her and she made grunting sounds in her sleep. She felt unhealthily soft, like cheap latex pillows.

I straddled her, leaned my weight on my elbows. I placed my hands on either side of her throat, thumbs together in front. I pressed, just a little.

She opened her eyes and said, "Darling . . ."

I made myself raise my thumbs, and then I crawled into my own head and walked around there for a moment, opening doors and looking inside, letting things sort themselves out.

Puzzled, "Darling?"

So I threw it to her a second time, a more symbolic and less permanent ritual of murder, and she heaved and bucked and perspired and moaned. I wouldn't let her go back to sleep afterward. I made her get up and dressed, and I drove her to where her car was parked and helped her open the door and sag behind the wheel. She drove off, weaving all over the road, and I figured it was about even odds that she would kill herself on the way home.

The smell of her was all over the room. I opened doors and windows, stripped the sheet from the bed, then went and stood under the shower for a long time. When I came back the air was cold but cleaner. I put the sheet on the bed upside down and killed the light. I got into bed. The pillow reeked of her hair spray, so I tossed it across the room and slept without it.

There had been no pleasure in it, not in the anticipation or the execution or now, in the memory.

No women exc. whores if you have to.

She was not precisely a whore, and I hadn't had to, so that

did it. The slate was clean now. Since leaving the island I had broken all ten of my rules.

My final night on the island had been very inactive once Dattner avoided going down for the last time. I brought him over to the fire and wrapped him in blankets and poured corn into him. He filled in details in a flat monotone. He must have talked for half an hour. I heard it all in silence, and when he was done and the bottle close to empty I bedded him down in the shack and piled all the blankets on top of him. I stretched out on the beach, positive that it was going to be a sleepless night for me. But I was too well trained, and sleep came in less than ten minutes.

Two hours later, judging by the moon, I was awake again. My body was wet with perspiration and shook with chills. I could smell myself. I try to stay out of the water at night, but now I waded in up to my knees and splashed myself clean. I toweled dry and sat down to think about things.

The operation wasn't bad. It had every chance in the world of turning sour, but what didn't? The real question was whether or not I wanted to get involved.

I could probably use the money, but that wasn't the point, either.

Then I played with the question of whether or not my life on the island needed an occasional change of pace. I went to Clint's every sixth day, and not solely because that was how long a dozen eggs lasted. I needed the human contact involved. Maybe I also needed periodic doses of another sort of contact and involvement. Or, on the other hand, maybe this was another temptation, another vestigial complication that had to be suppressed until it stopped making periodic noises.

I took a stick and sketched in the sand with it. I had a lot of lines furrowed before I realized I was roughing out a map of the Sprayhorn area. I started plotting movements on it, but that didn't make sense because I had no real picture of the terrain or the installations or anything else. I smoothed out the sand and put the stick down.

The Army was shipping the gear south in four trucks. There were two rumors—that it would be retained in Tampa for fast delivery to good-guy guerrillas if that policy was ever adopted, or that it had already been adopted and Tampa was just a way-station. Either way, the goods would be en route somewhere between the 3rd and 12th of February.

That was all we really knew. The trucks might move out in a convoy or one by one. They could be almost any size, or different sizes. Each one would have a driver and a guard in the cab; there might be men in back, there might not. And there might be aerial reconnaissance scheduled, and there might be armored cars leading and backing up, and so on.

We would have me on the inside, finding out things, and George on the outside, setting things up. The odds sounded ridiculous but he was right, it was feasible. You couldn't prove it with a computer. Not enough of the data was available, let alone suitable for programming.

But it could be done. That much I knew intuitively. It was the hows that took study. I ran a lot of the obvious variables through my mind and picked up some of the more likely problems and played at solving them. I was surprised how well my mind was handling the situation. I was thinking very clearly, getting a lot worked out. Of course it was all academic now, but I couldn't go back to sleep, and—

By sunrise, with the orange sun sitting fat and happy on indigo water, I knew there was no decision to make. The decision had been long made for me. Because for hours now I had not thought at all about the *whether*, but only about the *how*. The decision made itself while I was looking the other way.

I made two cans of coffee and split the remaining shine between them. I gave Goerge's can the best of it, figuring he would need it. I carried his coffee to the shack, shook him awake. He was alert instantly, a good sign. I gave him his coffee, and while he gulped it I told him I was in.

We were off the island by noon.

We spent the hours until then talking. Good talk this time,

crisp and clear, no interruptions, no cuteness, nothing in the way. We would make a part of a plan and fix it firmly and permanently in our minds, but at the same time we avoided getting married to any of our plans—whenever one of us spotted a hitch somewhere, we backed off and checked connections all the way down the line. Everything was loose and flexible and hypothetical, with more if-this-then-that then a twelve-horse parley. It had to be that way because of the glut of unknown factors. But at the same time these hours were more time than we would have together until the play was halfway home, and we had to get as much communicating out of the way now as possible.

It wasn't non-stop talking. We broke twice to swim and once to race around the island. I beat him with no trouble, but he was in better shape than I might have guessed, and this was another good omen.

We worked out codes and schedules. The first hurdle was making do with as little communication as possible. By the middle of the day he said he couldn't think of anything else, and neither could I.

"We'll go over the rest of it on the boat," he said. "I've got most of your things aboard. Clothes and all, ID. The pictures I used of you showed you in a crew cut. And no beard, of course. And no tan, but that doesn't matter in a picture. We can get your fingerprints in place aboard ship."

"You took a lot for granted."

"No, not really. It was a time problem, Paul. I couldn't find out first and then start building a depth cover for you. If you weren't what I wanted, or if you wouldn't play, I was out a couple of thousand. It's like putting a dime on a number, the odds are so long you don't cry if you never hit. Let's go."

"Go on ahead. It'll take me a few minutes."

"Take your time."

I did little clean-up jobs until he was well out of sight. Then I unburied my money belt and put it on. It was lighter now. I left a couple of thousand in the hole, neatly wrapped in a triple thickness of aluminum foil along with my personal papers and my list. When I took down the list I thought of the moonshine I'd added to my morning coffee, and the breakfast and lunch I hadn't had, and everything else.

I left my unbaited lines in the water. The third fish, which we hadn't eaten, was beginning to smell. I left it where it lay. The tides would deposit dead fish all over my island while I was gone. There would be no one around to throw them out to sea. The birds would eat some of them, the tide would take some away, and the rest would rot.

I went to the boat. He was standing alongside it smoking a cigarette. We shoved it free of its moorings and got in. The engine caught first try, and I stood in the bow and looked where I was going, not where I had been.

More talk and more plans. He was going to run the boat straight down to Key West and let the owner send a cab for it. I would have to shave on the boat; he had a battery-razor I could use. It wouldn't work on my beard, but he also had a safety razor and a can of lather. I managed to get all but an eighth inch of stubble that way, then used the electric to eat up the rest.

From Key West you can fly to Miami. I let him have the first plane out and agreed to take the next one. By the time I got to Miami he would be somewhere over the Carolinas.

We went over everything a last time, and it looked tight.

"One thing," he said. "Last night, when I kept going underwater." He made it sound light enough but that only showed that he was good at the game. "I didn't know you would get that rough, of course. Or that you would have bought the straight story to begin with. But the part that gets me is this—you were *supposed* to spot holes in my opening story. I allowed for that, I set it up. If you hadn't tumbled I would have found a way to make it even more obvious."

"I'm not surprised. You work that way, you like one cover on top of another. Layers."

"Wheels within wheels. It works, Paul. No, to get back to

it, I used the first pitch to set you up for the second. That was the real curve ball, and you didn't even bother tearing it up. You tore me up instead."

"So?"

"I thought it was a fairly solid story."

"I suppose it was."

"And one two three and I'm in the middle of the ocean. What tipped you off? How did you know I was lying?"

"I didn't."

"You—"

"I figured if you stuck to it through three duckings it was true, and if you changed it you would come up with the straight thing. It was a cheap investment." I smiled. "Like buying clothes for me and setting up my cover in advance. Same thing. Give a little to get a lot."

He gave me a lot of silence. Then he told me he was glad we were on the same team. So was I.

NINE

THE MORNING AFTER I wished T.J. Morrison a happy birthday, I received a return telegram at my office in the compound. It was coded, a box cipher constructed upon the key word *Superman*, with the additional complication of a letters-for-numbers substitution cipher to back it up. I don't think anyone on base could have cracked it, and doubt if anyone thought of trying, but this is what they would have read:

BUYER SET PRICE FIRM BAKER FOUR NINETEEN HOWARD
CARSON CAMERON TWO.

The first four words meant that our outlet was prepared to take delivery at our price. Baker four nineteen was a rendezvous—I should meet him at seven P.M. at the second of our proposed meeting places on the fourth day following. Meanwhile, in two days I could reach him with a wire to Howard Carson at the Hotel Cameron.

I burned the telegram, along with the three sheets of paper used to decode it. Then I left my office and wandered around the area trying not to look too much like a spy. After a day of this the word got out, and the base personnel went to great lengths to ignore me when I meandered into their areas of responsibility.

Local security was not as weak as I had expected. General Baldwin Winden might be a clown, but the base ran itself fairly well in spite of his hand at the helm. No vehicle went in or out of the main gate without getting close scrutiny from the guard. On the inside, each of the concrete block buildings had its own informal security set-up. You didn't need a pass to go from Point A to Point B, but if there was no obvious motive for the trip, someone was likely to take a second look at you. This happened to me the first day, until the word got around that I was a civilian snooper, and from then on I felt like the invisible man.

It didn't take too long to find out where the goods were being stored for shipment, and how they were guarded, and just how much space they occupied. Nor was it difficult to pick out the on-post intelligence types. They didn't quite wear signs, but they might as well have. I kept moving, kept noticing things, and spent my night adding up all the bits and pieces and making a total picture out of them. It was a little like working a jigsaw puzzle—I wouldn't know exactly where we were until the last piece went into place, but the closer I got, the better idea I had. I was learning things that cut down our variables, and the comforting thing was that no obvious flaw in our basic planning had yet emerged.

After four days of this, I left the base around dinner time and drove to Pierre. It's pronounced "peer," it's the capital of the state, and it has an airport which George's wire called *Baker*.

He was in a booth at the coffee shop when I got there. I sat in the booth next to his and ordered a hamburger and coffee.

He said, "I have forty minutes between planes. Everything going good?"

"So far."

"Did the MI people show?"

"No."

"Good. They'll be here at least three days before D-Day. Probably two of them. Today's what? The 30th. If I had to bet right now, I'd say that they would ship on the 7th. I'll be on the spot and ready by the third, that's Monday."

"Not cutting it too close?"

"I don't think so. What have you got?"

"A hundred small things. I've been—" I dropped it when I saw the waitress coming, waited until she was out of range again. Then, talking at my coffee cup, I said, "I've been keeping busy. The goods are all being stored in one spot. They haven't been loaded yet, but I've got the carriers pinpointed. Four trucks, each about the size of a troop carrier. Say a capacity of 2500 cubic feet, top. That checks with my rough guess on the goods themselves. They could run ten thousand, but no more."

"That's already a little more than we figured."

"A little. Trucks are armor-plated. They look like big Brinks trucks. They're empty now, and I'm positive they're scheduled to haul the stuff."

"Uh-huh."

I drank some coffee. "We have to wait until they load and ship. To take them off now, we'd need ten good men and a lot of luck. Most important, we wouldn't have any lead time. Those roads are rotten, most of them. We would only have one way out of Sprayhorn, we'd never make it."

"Go on, Paul."

"I sketched the next part. I'll give you the drawing later, or do you want it now?"

"Later's fine."

"All right. They'll have to go south from the post. There's only one decent road and they'll all have to take it. Now, here's the problem—I get the impression from the general that the four trucks are going to four different places. One to Florida, one to Massachusetts, one to Texas and one to the Coast. California."

"Oh, shit."

"Right. He could be wrong, he's no genius, but I think he knows something we didn't know. That's why I tried to find some way to pull it off inside, when everything would be in one place. Once those trucks start off on separate roads—"

"Uh-huh."

"But there's a stretch of fifteen miles that they'll all have to take. If they were going in a convoy all the way to Florida, we could pick our spot. But we can't count on that."

"So we have to hit them within fifteen miles of home."

"It's the only safe way. Unless you want to settle for one load."

"The hell with that." He fell silent, and I worked on my hamburger. Then he asked how certain I was that they would all leave the post at the same time. I told him I wasn't certain, but it was the way I would do it if I were setting it up.

"Why? Makes them a sitting duck, doesn't it?"

"Yes and no. Remember, they wouldn't worry that someone would want all four trucks. They would just want to make sure that nothing happened to *any* of the trucks. And they would realize that the tight part is on the road leading south from the post. After that, on larger highways, they would have less to worry about. So that's where they would want to use a convoy. In unity is strength, all of that."

"You'll have to confirm that."

"I know."

"And find out what kind of contact they'll use. They may send some cars along to ride shotgun."

"Or aerial surveillance."

"Christ, I hope not. Ten thousand cubic feet, that's more than I thought. We'll need two very big trucks, won't we?"

"Or a van. I have a few ideas, George."

"Let's hear them."

I talked for a long time, and he listened, and again we worked together very well. He found a few holes in my approach, but they were not as bad as they might have been, and by the time he was ready to get on his plane I felt good about the way things were shaping up.

"Just stay on top of it for now," he said. "When the MI boys show up, that's when you'll get more of an idea of specifics. They'll be able to tell you just how the whole operation is going to be staged."

"They'll also check me out a lot harder than General Baldy Windy."

"That's no problem."

"Oh?"

"Your Agency card is a real one, Paul. That's the thing to remember. All they can do is ask the Agency if you really exist, and all the Agency can do is say no. But that's what we always say regardless, and MI knows it. They can't possibly poke a hole in your cover."

"They might have my prints on file somewhere."

"So? They'll establish that your real name isn't Lynch and that you have a good service record. So what? They'd get the same line if you really were an Agency man. Once the job's pulled off you might be hot under your own name, but that's a name and identity you got rid of long before you found your little island and went native. You hadn't counted on being Paul Kavanagh again, I hope?"

"No."

"Then what's the problem?"

"There isn't any," I agreed. "Have a good flight."

That was the 30th of January, a Thursday. Saturday morning I was at my desk when the phone rang. It was the general's secretary. Would I please report to the valiant leader at once?

There were two men in his office. They were both majors, unless their ranks were as spurious as my own. Gen. Winden was standing stiffly alongside his desk. "Well, well, well," he said. "Mr. Richard John Lynch, may I present Maj. Philip Bourke and Maj. Lawrence O'Gara. Mr. Lynch is a civilian intelligence officer," he told them, "and I'm sure the three of you gentlemen will have a great deal to talk about. Since the powers that be do not seem to feel that Fort Joshua Tree is

capable of handling its own affairs, I'm reassured to know
that three fine men will keep matters under control. Indeed,
gentlemen. Indeed, reassured!''

I looked at Bourke and O'Gara and they looked at me, and
the general looked at all three of us. Bourke, the older of the
two, started to say something, then changed his mind. They
seemed rather dismayed at the whole affair. I could understand this, and suggested they might want to come to my
office for a moment. They threw salutes at the general and
followed me out of there.

When we were all three in my cubicle, with the door shut,
Bourke heaved himself into a chair and sighed. ''I heard
about that overstuffed son of a bitch,'' he said, ''but it's
nothing to seeing him in the flesh. Words do not begin. He
wasn't supposed to tell us about you, was he?''

''It wasn't what the office had in mind,'' I admitted.

''A shame you had to tell him who you were in the first
place. He never would have worked it out on his own.''

''You might be right.''

O'Gara said, ''You should see his record. You wouldn't
believe it.'' His voice was Boston Irish. ''But if he were any
good they wouldn't have sent us here. He gave us a story to
explain your interest in this one, Lynch, but I couldn't make
sense of it.''

I told him it didn't make much sense to me, either. ''The
eventual destination of the shipment comes under Agency
auspices, that's all I know. So we're showing some unofficial
interest down the line. That's about all.''

''Expecting trouble?''

''Not that I know of.'' I looked at him, then turned to study
Bourke. ''Why? Something in the air?''

''We wouldn't know. If they had to send us here, why
couldn't they wait until maybe August? A week in this town,
I don't know. What do you do for kicks?''

We did fifteen minutes on various ways of amusing oneself
in Sprayhorn. I was waiting for the pitch, and I wasn't
surprised when they made it casual. Bourke said something

about the general having simplified things, and that it was just as well our identities were out in the open. We might help each other, we could give each other company, and otherwise we'd have spent all our time running checks on each other.

"Amen to that," O'Gara said. "And just for the record, Comrade Richard, here's my Red Party Card."

He gave me a leatherette case about the size of a passport. It had his picture—I think it was his picture, but it didn't come all that close—and a thumbprint and description. I made a show of giving it a careful look-see while pretending to pass it with a glance. Then Bourke produced his ID and I had to glance-examine it, too.

"And now, friends, we make the party complete." The first thing I handed them was the Maj. John Walker paraphernalia. Bourke said it wasn't bad work, but O'Gara didn't think it would fool anyone who looked hard at it. Then I gave them the Agency ticket in the Lynch name. O'Gara hardly looked at it before passing it on to Bourke, who took a quick glance and flipped it back to me. There was just the quietest click when O'Gara photographed it. They were pretty smooth.

"Major Walker himself," O'Gara said. "John Walker."

"None other."

"I used to know a bottle by that name. Do they call you Red Label, by any chance?"

"Sounds subversive. Now Black Label, that's something else again. If you old soldiers would care to pursue the matter, there's a research center just this side of town that I could recommend—"

We went to a roadhouse together and did some fairly serious drinking. When I came back from the john one time my glass was a little sticky in spots with what I guessed was scotch tape residue; now they would have some prints to compare with their photograph of my ID. According to George, it wouldn't matter if they sent the prints to Washington. I hoped they wouldn't bother.

With that out of the way, we all three relaxed and made a

day out of it. We went to another place for a late lunch and
then returned to the first roadhouse and sat drinking until the
crowd from the base arrived around the dinner hour. I got the
impression that they didn't have anything resembling final
orders yet, so I didn't bother pumping them very hard. They
seemed interested in learning the final destination of the
weapons, but I was vague on that score, so they gathered
either that I didn't know or that I wouldn't tell, whereupon
they let go of it. They were pretty decent types, especially
O'Gara, who had an unsuaully dry sense of humor for a
career officer. Bourke ran a little closer to type, but was still
good company.

I had to drink a little heavier than I wanted to, but I stayed
on top of the liquor. I left them around six-thirty, stopped in
town to send George a prearranged telegram, then went back
to the motel.

Something woke me before sunrise Sunday, a backfiring
truck or a bad dream. I got dressed and went out. The snow
that had held off for a few days was coming down again, and
according to the car radio it would do so for a long while. I ate
breakfast and drank a lot of coffee, then went back to the
motel. I didn't stay there long, though, because I had the
feeling that Bourke and O'Gara might pay a call, and I didn't
want to see them now. I got back in the car and went out to
look things over.

I drove to the base, then went on past it, tracing the route
the four trucks would take from Fort Tree south. It was only a
fifteen-mile stretch, but with the snow coming down hard it
took me the better part of two hours to run the length of it and
back. In all that time, I only saw two other cars, both of them
civilian. The day and hour may have had something to do
with it, of course. We couldn't count on the traffic being that
light during the week.

The countryside itself was flat and barren in all directions,
large farms and open fields. The view would probably have

been monotonous enough under any circumstances, but with snow everywhere there was really nothing at all to look at. Now and then a farmhouse or barn broke the barren whiteness of the view.

I drove to the end and back, stopping periodically to check my mileage and make notes of likely spots. If we were going to take the trucks, we had to pick our spot carefully. We needed a stretch of several hundred yards away from houses and side roads, a spot where we could make the touch without being seen, a spot we could seal to traffic easily and effectively. I found three possibilities on the way out and eliminated one of them on the way back.

That left two, and either one was better than I'd expected and a little less than I'd hoped for. They were 4.3 and 11.2 miles from the base, which meant that one was too close to the beginning of the run and the other too close to the end. My third choice had been ideal in that respect, right smack in the middle, but on the way back I had noticed a secondary road that fed right into it at its midpoint, and that seemed enough to rule it out.

In the motel room, I used my notes and my memory to rough out a map of the fifteen-mile route. I drew it to scale and noted all the landmarks I could remember in the areas of the two ambush sites. I played with the map for an hour or so. When it stopped snowing I went out in the car again and had another look at the route. This time I stopped at every access road and filled it in on the map. I also added as many of the houses and barns as possible, redrafted to show bends and curves in the road, and made other notations for contour. This last was hardly worth the trouble. The ground was so flat that dips in the road hardly entered into things at all. To the west, on the other side of the Missouri, were the Black Hills and the Badlands and all of that. But here everything was flat.

I went to a bar that night but couldn't relax at all. My mind was on the two ambush sites and I couldn't turn it off. I went back to the motel and dragged out the map again, bouncing a variety of plan elements off it, seeing what would work and what wouldn't, trying to guess in advance the elements we hadn't allowed for.

It was a waste of time, but there was time to waste and my mind wouldn't stay focused on anything else. When I managed to turn it aside I found myself thinking about other things, more troublesome things. George was arriving the following night, and from that time on it would be pressure all the way; in the meanwhile it wouldn't do to get hung up on uncomfortable thoughts.

I put the map in my money belt before I went to sleep, and slept with it fastened tightly about my middle.

TEN

ON MONDAY MORNING they started loading the trucks.

There was no memo to that effect on my desk. The only thing on my desk when I got there was a coded wire from George, and all it said once I unscrambled it was UNDERDOG, which meant he'd be in Aberdeen that night. For all that, it hardly had to be in code. You can take the man out of the Agency but you can't take the Agency out of the man. George was incurable.

The decoding process, as it happened, almost kept me from discovering about the loading operation. I finished destroying the wire and my work sheets and went outside just in time to see one of the four armored cars disappearing into a building, the very building in which the shipment was presently stored. I waited, but no other trucks showed up, and I wondered if they were going to load and ship them one by one. If that was the case, we were in all kinds of trouble.

I headed for the warehouse and was halfway there when Larry O'Gara emerged from it and waved at me. He trotted over to me. "Nothing to see," he told me. "Phil's inside watching them load. They're on truck number three, and when you've seen one, etc. Christ, it's cold. Is it like this all winter long?''

"I'm a stranger here myself."

"A few more days and we can all add this to our list of happy memories. Let's get inside."

We went to my office. It was still smoky from the telegram I had incinerated, but if O'Gara noticed he kept it to himself. "They'll keep the loaded trucks inside until they take off," he said. "We'll go over later and have a look."

"Fine with me."

He lit a cigarette, then leaned back and put his feet on my desk. "We got some messages from home this morning," he said.

"Word from on high?"

"Uh-huh. Phil will brief you when he gets here. Right now he's making himself dispensable. The right crates have to go on the right trucks, and the labels with 'This Side Up' have to face up, and he seems to think none of this will come about unless he hangs in there. Funny guy."

"With Baldy in command, I can understand his logic."

"Oh, I don't know. The apes who haul things around seem competent, no matter who's in command." He flicked ashes on my floor. "The Texas truck was loaded first, and that was the important one, so I don't see why he's still there. He'll be along any minute. Looked for you yesterday, incidentally."

"Oh?"

"At your motel. We found a fellow named Carr, a light colonel who talks a fair game of bridge. Thought you might make a fourth. I think you said the other day that you play?"

"I'm rusty. I've been away from it five years."

"You didn't get a bridge game in Brazil?"

"The only bridge I ever saw was one we kept building and somebody kept blowing up. I wore out a deck of cards playing solitaire, but that was about the extent of it."

"It would all come back to you."

"I suppose so."

"But you weren't at your room, so the point never came

up. What did you do, have yourself a sightseeing tour of beautiful South Dakota?''

"Something like that." I wondered if this was maybe a little too casual to be true. "Practiced my snow driving," I said.

"Oh?"

Far too casual. "And did a little homework in the process," I admitted. "I thought it might not be a bad idea to check the roads south of here. I still don't know how I fit into the picture on this operation, but I figured it wouldn't hurt to get some idea of the terrain. Just in case the office decides to put me on active duty."

His face changed ever so slightly, just enough to tell me I'd made the right answer. Then he started to tell me something about Carr and his crazy wife, and told me just enough so that I had the feeling it was Col. Carr's wife who had helped me break Rule #4. That was fine, it would give me an excuse to avoid future bridge games.

"A really strange gal," he was saying. "I got the impression . . ." But I didn't find out what impression he had gotten, because then the door opened and Bourke came in. He looked at O'Gara, and O'Gara nodded, and Bourke closed the door and found his way into a chair. The three of us talked about how cold it was, and they did a routine on the practice of locating army posts in uninhabitable areas. Their timing was good enough for me to suspect this was a bit they had refined over the years.

"All loaded," Bourke said eventually. "Larry tell you about it, Dick?"

"Just that the trucks will stay there until they're ready to roll them."

"Uh-huh. Your truck is number two, incidentally."

"I already told him," Larry said.

"Told me what?"

"That the Texas truck is second. Come off it. Don't be cute, or haven't they told you? My spies say you got a telegram today."

"I did, but this is the first I've heard of Texas."

He looked at me appraisingly. "What are your orders, exactly?"

"Hardly anything specific so far. Just stay on the scene and keep an eye on the departure of the shipment."

"You weren't told to take an interest in any particular truck?"

"No. Not yet, at least. Why?"

They looked at each other. Then Larry said, "I don't see why you'd be cagy, so all I can guess is that our team's a day ahead of you on this one. It's about time. I think I'll declare a military victory."

"I don't—"

"On the other hand, maybe they don't want to tell you until the last minute, or you'll be mad at getting sent here."

"I'm that already. They say you get used to the cold, but they say that about hanging, too. What the hell are you talking about, Larry?"

He lit another cigarette. "There's supposed to be a play made for one of the trucks," he said finally. "The usual sort of scuttlebutt. According to what we've got, a group of super-patriots want to take possession of the armaments so that they'll be able to prevent the Russians from sending a gunboat up the Rio Grande. You know the drift. Some of those Texas left-wingers—"

"Right-wingers," Bourke said.

"Did I say left? I meant right. The Sons of '76 or '69 or some such number. A paramilitary group. Listen, you can save me a lot of excess words if you already know all this."

"I've heard of the group but I don't know anything about them fitting into this operation."

"Really?"

"Really."

"Good enough. The word is that they're based in Texas, and they plan to make an ambush attempt on the truck heading for Amarillo. You know one of the trucks is going to Amarillo?"

"To be honest, all I knew was Texas."

"Well, the precise destination is Amarillo. These jokers are supposed to have an intercept scheduled somewhere between the moment we ship the goods and the moment they arrive there. Which means, of course, that they'll hit it somewhere in Texas. Amarillo's less than a hundred miles from the Oklahoma line, so they won't have much room to work in."

"Unless they hit it in Oklahoma," Bourke said.

"Which wouldn't make sense. They don't want to cross a state line."

"If they're crazy enough to do it, what difference does a state line make?" O'Gara laughed. "Either way it sounds like a load of shit, but nowadays any load of shit with Texas in it seems to inspire belief. Anyway, Dick, that's where you come into the picture."

"In Texas?" I didn't honestly have to pretend to be confused. I *was* confused.

"Texas is where the rest of your buddies are. You, lucky man, got sent here to guard the North Pole."

"What Larry's getting at," Phil said, "is that evidently the Sons of '69—"

"I think it's '76, actually—"

"Whatever they are, these Sons of Something must be one of the groups of clowns on your list. Though usually the Bureau gets them, don't they?"

It seemed time for me to say something. "We keep an eye on certain crackpot groups," I said. "Insofar as they have foreign contacts or impinge on foreign policy—"

"Uh-huh. Well, that's the drift, then. Getting the goods to Amarillo is a military job, and we're handling it. But making sure that the Sons don't get their hands on them is evidently an Agency job as well, and a team of your gang is supposed to be on the spot in Texas already. We're arranging the route to minimize the danger of an ambush once the Texas border is crossed. And you're here to keep your eyes open and freeze your balls off, and if we weren't stuck here too, Dick, I might go so far as to feel sorry for you.''

It wasn't hard to give them the right reaction. By the time he finished his speech, I was really angry. I must have gotten a wire crossed mentally, to the point where I believed for a moment or two that we were really going to ambush the truck in Texas, and that George had shafted me by sending me to Sprayhorn. That's a recognized hazard in any sort of role-playing. Anyone good enough to operate under cover has a certain amount of trouble keeping the cover separated from the reality in his own mind. In this case it worked out for the better. I showed the right degree of annoyance at the way I was being called upon to waste my time and comfort, and Bourke and O'Gara had a laugh at my expense, and I joined in.

''If they were shipping sheep shit from Texas to South Dakota,'' I said, ''then guess who'd be on the receiving end that time.''

''They'll never do it. This place has all the sheep shit it needs.''

''The Army wouldn't care.''

There was a knock at the door, and a non-com came in with a telegram for me. ''Now's when they tell you about it,'' O'Gara said. I agreed, and put the telegram in my pocket without opening it.

''Come on,'' Bourke said, ''we'll take a look at the trucks. Now that you know how important they are, you might want to see how we're setting it up.''

It was cold on the way over and just as cold inside the storage depot. The building wasn't heated. All four trucks stood in line at the far end of the building, away from the big doorway. We walked over to them, and Bourke pointed out the one destined for Amarillo. He called a soldier over and ordered him to unlock the back.

''Our idea,'' he explained. ''We shifted the load, apportioned a few cases among the three other trucks.''

''Won't that screw things up?''

O'Gara shook his head. "We shifted goods the truck was heavy on," he said. "Some chemical stuff that'll never see use anywhere, and some of the gas grenades. We've corrected the invoices accordingly, so that no one in Amarillo will start raising hell. They can always adjust quantities later on, ship stuff from other bases to Amarillo, but I don't really think they'll bother."

"Probably not," Bourke agreed. "The important thing is that we've made room in this truck for four men armed with M-14s. That's plenty of insurance, don't you think?"

"Uh-huh. They ride in back?"

"Right. They'll get bumped around, but that's army life for you. If any crackpot patriots open this rig before the truck gets to Amarillo, they won't even know what hit them."

"Beautiful."

"Of course there'll be an armed man sitting next to the driver all the way," O'Gara said. "The same as the other three."

"And we'll follow this one down."

"In a car?"

He nodded. "We'll keep all four trucks together as far as Omaha. At that point number one heads due east, number three swings southeast, and number four goes west to California. Our baby keeps on going south and we ride her tail all the way home." He grinned at me. "We've got a sheaf of maps where we're bedded down. If you want to come along, we'll give you a quick briefing on the route."

We took their car, and it wasn't hard to spot it as government issue; it was the current year's Ford, the bottom of the line, with absolutely no extras. Not even an ashtray. Their quarters were on the base, a single squat concrete block cube designed by the same imaginative genius who had created the rest of the base.

We spread maps on O'Gara's bed and the two of them took turns explaining the proposed route to me. I had to pay closest attention to the part that interested me least, the route of the Texas-bound truck after the convoy broke up in Omaha. The part I cared about they covered in a few words, and it was as I had figured; the four trucks would move together along the fifteen-mile stretch. After that it all became academic as far as I was concerned.

But I had to pretend to pay attention. "Now here's where we go a few extra miles," Phil Bourke showed me. "From Omaha, the most natural route would take us almost due southwest toward Amarillo. But instead we're routing the truck along the Missouri as far as Kansas City, Kansas. Then we head straight down to Tulsa, then over to Oklahoma City. Get the point? The roads are bigger and better, and they have more traffic. I don't think they'd be fool enough to try anything north of the Texas line, but this makes it just that much safer."

I agreed that this made a lot of sense.

"There are two ways to bring the goods through to Amarillo. We can come due south through Stratford and Moore or cut in from the east through Canadian, Pampa and White Deer. That way's a little longer, but again we take advantage of better roads. Also, we'll be picking up two escort jeeps in Fort Jeffrey Hillary just east of the border, see? And by the time—"

I let them give me the full rundown, and I asked most of the right questions. They weren't making provision for air cover; that would be handled by the receiving unit out of Amarillo. All four trucks would receive air spotting throughout the trip once they separated in Omaha.

Finally they finished and asked me how it looked, and I said it looked airtight to me. No questions? Just one, I said, and they couldn't answer it—where did I fit in?

"The answer's probably in your pocket, Dick."

"How's that?"

"Your telegram. You figure they'll send you along?"

"Damned if I know. I can't see the point myself."

"It's a long trip, if they make you take your own car. At least the boys in the trucks will be splitting the driving, and so will Phil and I in our car. Maybe they'll let you ride with us.''

We all laughed at that. They drove me back to my office, and on the way I asked the question that had been on my mind for most of the past hour. "Not that I'm complaining," I said, "but how come you brought me in on all this?"

They glanced quickly at each other, then at me. "No reason not to," Larry said. "We aren't telling you anything you won't know anyway."

"True, but—"

"And inter-service rivalry doesn't quite enter the picture this time, does it? We're no saints, we hate to see you boys grab all the glory, but there's not going to be any glory in this one, not up here in South Dakota. The trucks leave here on schedule. If the Texas truck arrives on time, that's routine. If somebody makes a play for it, then whoever's on the spot can be glorious. And if a long shot comes through and the crackpots pull it off, they won't be passing out glory. They'll be pouring out shit with a ladle.''

"Oh," I said.

Larry O'Gara grinned. "So naturally we want you in on the planning," he said. "You'll be one more person for them to pour the shit on.''

I went to my office and closed the door. I opened the telegram. For the first time it wasn't even coded. It said SCRATCH UNDERDOG SIT TIGHT.

I still had the telegram in my hand when the door opened. It was O'Gara. "We just got one of those ourselves," he said. "I hope to Christ I never become a general. I'd hate to spend my declining years acting like an idiot. Did you get the same news we got?"

"I don't know," I said. I decided the hell with it and handed him the wire. "You tell me," I said.

He read it. "Uh-huh. Well, that's half of it. *Underdog* meant the original shipping date, right?"

It didn't, but I nodded.

"You'll probably get the rest in a few minutes, unless your people don't have it yet. You knew if course that shipping date was Thursday."

"I don't recall anybody mentioning it."

"No, we didn't tell you and you didn't tell us. Actually we took it for granted that you knew, and you realize how secrecy becomes a habit in this game. Well, they moved it up."

"Wednesday?"

He shook his head. "Tomorrow morning. Six hundred thirty hours." He heaved a sigh. "Phil's on the line now trying to change their minds for them. We haven't even lined up our drivers yet, let alone the four clowns who'll sit in back with the M-14s. I told Phil he was wasting his time."

"Six-thirty," I said.

"That's the word. That's what? Twenty hours from now? Not even that." He shook his head. "Got to go. Let me know when you get the word. If they tell you a different time, for God's sake let me hear about it."

He left, drawing the door shut after him. I burned the telegram and dropped the ashes in the wastebasket. *Scratch underdog sit tight.* The score was less than twenty hours away and Dattner's arrival was scrambled, and I was supposed to sit tight.

I got in the car and went to the motel. I lay down on the bed and looked at the ceiling. When in doubt, do nothing.

That was where I was, and that was what I did.

ELEVEN

I MUST HAVE called the base half a dozen times just to find out if there were any messages for me. There never were. The last time, around five-thirty, I had them get hold of Bourke for me. He wanted to know what I'd heard from my office. I told him they hadn't given me a thing since I talked to O'Gara.

"We've had confirmation," he said. "We roll at six-thirty in the morning. All appeals denied. I don't like it."

"Neither do I."

"I don't even like being awake at that hour, but what I like least of all is all this hurry-up action. This morning I figured we were going through a lot of waste motion, but now I'm not so sure. I've got a feeling there's going to be trouble in Texas."

"You could be right."

"No other explanation, Dick. I don't like it."

He couldn't have liked it less than I did. The way I saw it there were two possibilities, and one was worse than the other. With the shipment heading south at sunrise and George taking himself out of the play, at best we were letting the score slip past us.

That was the best way to look at it. Another possibility, and one that seemed increasingly likely the more thought I gave it, was that our play was already completely blown. Somehow or other they had tipped to us. That explained the new departure date, and it also explained why I had never gotten a second wire from George. They didn't let you send telegrams from a jail cell.

I couldn't sit still. I kept getting up and pacing around like a caged wolf. I did several crazy things. Once I started packing, and I had one suitcase half filled before realizing that there was nothing I wanted to take with me. I put everything back where it belonged. Another time I decided that I had to make a run for it, and I went out and took the car a mile down the road before I managed to get hold of myself and drive back to the motel.

Obviously my cover hadn't been blown so far, or they would have ordered a pickup for me at the same time as they changed the shipping date. It was possible that they had George; if so, he would talk, but I would have a few hours safe time. I compromised with myself. I stayed at the motel, but instead of walking back and forth across the room I sat in my car and listened to the radio while the sky got dark.

I was parked off to the side, lights and motor off. A few minutes before eight a car turned into the lot and moved slowly past the units, as if the driver was trying to find a particular number. The light was coming from the wrong direction and I couldn't see the driver's face.

The car stopped next to my unit. I decided it was either George or someone who had come to arrest me. The door opened and the driver got out, and it was George. I winked my headlights at him as he knocked on my door. He turned around slowly. He had his hand inside his coat. He didn't draw the gun, but he didn't take his hand out, either. Maybe he was posing as Napoleon.

I snapped off the lights and flicked on the dome light so that he could see my face. He nodded and withdrew his hand, and I got out of the car and hurried over to him. "We'll take my car," he said. "It's stolen, I don't want to leave it parked."

"You want to cruise around in it?"

"Don't argue, just get in." I did, and he slid behind the wheel. The car was a Chrysler with all the extras, including air-conditioning, which was the last thing we needed. He backed up, swung out of the lot and took a left away from town.

"They switched the takeoff time," he said.

"I know. Six-thirty tomorrow morning."

"I didn't have time to put it in a wire. I didn't even have time to code what I sent you. I got that wire off from the airport and ran for my plane. Those rotten bastards."

"What happened?"

"Crazy bastards. I've had some day. You know where I'm supposed to be right now?"

"Amarillo."

"How did you know?"

"I guessed. They seem to expect some sort of right-wing nut group to take the Texas truck between the Oklahoma line and Amarillo. I just heard this today, and just a few minutes before everything started to fall in. Give me the whole thing, will you?"

"Sure." He took a breath. "I think it's all blown."

"Just let me hear it. And slow down, these roads are pure hell in this weather."

"You're telling me? I put this oversized piece of crud in two ditches so far. I stole it in Chicago. Did you ever steal a car right off the street? I'll tell you, Paul—"

"Calm down."

"Right." He slowed the car, stayed silent for a full minute. When he started talking again his voice was pitched lower and the brittle quality was gone.

He said, "Okay, let's start at the beginning. The crap about the Sons of the Spirit of '76 was my doing."

"I thought it was."

"It seemed like a sensible diversion. We talked about

something like that. After you told me about the trucks splitting up, I found out the Texas destination and got some rumors in motion. I figured it would be good to get them concentrated on protecting one truck. Then if they got any other rumors they would fit them into the framework I had established. You follow?'' I nodded. "What I didn't count on was the Sons of the Spirit getting hold of the leak. It's not certain that they did, but the way it shapes up they have a man planted either in our shop or in Military Intelligence, and I guess they heard the rumble and decided it was a good idea. Or else it was just a case of one rumor feeding on another. It's hard to say how these things work. I remember one time when—''

"Forget it.''

"Check. The upshot is that there's serious concern that the Texas truck will be hit, and I'd say there's a good chance of it. Either way, the Agency was ordered in on the play. A crew went to Texas today.'' He managed a smile. "Including yours truly.''

"Why didn't you go?''

"Because I'd rather have a million dollars.''

"You think we still have a shot at it?''

"Who knows? Right now I don't think anything. You want to hear something really funny, Paul? I quit smoking a week ago.''

"Why?''

"You told me yourself it's a dirty habit. No, seriously, I wanted to be in the best possible shape for this. And it wasn't hard to quit. It even looked good at the office. If I got nervous, I could always pass it off as smoker's nerves.'' He coughed, laughed. "For the first time since I quit I really want a cigarette.''

I waited for him to go on. He slowed the big car, turned left on a dirt road. I told him it didn't go anywhere. He said he could turn around eventually. I waited, and he turned around at the first driveway and headed back toward the main road.

I asked him what would happen when he didn't show in Amarillo.

"I can cover myself," he said.

"All right."

"Paul, we have less than twelve hours."

"More like ten."

"More like ten. Two more days and it might have been easy. Or as close to easy as it could ever get. I had a van lined up, I had some details worked out and ready to go—"

"Forget them now."

"Yeah. Did you manage to get any of their planning?"

"All of it."

"What?"

I told him how they had briefed me, and why.

"That's a big break," he said. "Give it to me now, all of it. I won't interrupt. Give me the whole thing."

I didn't give him everything because there was no point to it. I told him how they had it arranged and what precautions they would be taking from the moment of departure to the breakup of the four-truck convoy in Omaha. I told him about my own reconnaissance, and the spots I had tentatively selected for the ambush. He wasn't at his best. He was hyped up, and there were points he missed at first hearing that I had to explain to him a second time. When I was done he pulled over to the side of the road and told me to take the wheel.

"I want to go over the route now," he said. "I want to see the spots you're talking about."

We went back through the town and past the base. The landmarks I had pinpointed before disappeared in the darkness, but I remembered my mileage figures and found both locations without trouble.

On the way back he took a vial of pills from his breast pocket, swallowed two capsules without water, offered the tube to me. I asked what they were.

"Bennies," he said. "We'll be up all night."

"I don't want them."

"You'll need them later."

"Maybe."

He capped the vial. "Suit yourself," he said. "Let me know if you change your mind. If you feel yourself slipping, speak up."

I told him I would. He told me to drive back to the motel. I parked the Chrysler in the back. I started to get out, but he put his hand on my arm. He said my room probably wasn't bugged but he didn't want to take any chances. I agreed and said I wanted to get my maps. He told me to come back to the car.

The map was in my money belt but I hadn't wanted to flash it. I took it out in the room and put all the Walker and Lynch identification in it. Then I changed my mind and returned the Lynch card to my jacket pocket. I returned to the car and we sat there in the darkness. He left the dome light off and used a pencil flashlight to study the map.

"I like the second ambush point best," he said. "You know why?"

"No."

"More space between access roads. And it'll take them another ten or fifteen minutes to get there, and we need every extra minute we can get."

"Okay."

"We might pull this off, Paul. They've made it pretty easy, and then they complicated everything by screwing up the timing on us. And those four buggers with M-14s. I don't like those four buggers with M-14s."

"Neither do I."

"I had a van lined up but that's out. I had everything set. I had three long-haul movers booked for Thursday. They would come to an address in Pierre with their trucks empty, and they'd be tied up in a basement while I took their van. I booked three so that two of them could do a no-show and we'd still be covered."

"That's out now."

"Don't I know it. Wait a minute—"

I put a hand on his arm. "George," I said.

He didn't say anything.

"Just take it easy, George. Forget the elements that fell in. Let's start with now. There are certain things we need. We'll go over them one by one and find out what they are, and then we'll see if there's any way we can make it work."

"All right."

"We had a good thing planned but it's blown to hell and gone. We have to start in fresh and there's not much time."

"Right." He nodded slowly. "A van. Some highway signs, a couple planks and sawhorses. Forget guns. I've got a Thompson broken down in the back seat. In the suitcase. And a few extra handguns. Let's see now, we'll need—"

It was past nine when I got out of his stolen car and into my own rented one. I made myself forget how I felt about driving in snow and made the car do tricks all the way to Sioux Falls. It was a long drive, and it should have taken even longer than it did, but fortunately I had a maniac behind the wheel. I got in a fancy spinout once that almost took me off the road and into a tree, but the car somehow stayed on the road and I somehow got to Sioux Falls without getting killed.

I went to four trucking firms, plus four more that were closed for the night, before I found the man I was looking for. His name was Sprague, and his firm was Sprague Trucking Corp., and the sign on his desk said that this was a republic, not a democracy, and let's keep it that way.

Another sign, on the wall, said, "I have an agreement with Hoffa/He stays out of my office/and I stay out of his cell!"

He looked up at me over a desk piled high with papers. He was a big man gone to fat, with a flushed face and a lot of unruly white hair. His beard stubble was white mixed with gray. He was wearing a white shirt with the sleeves rolled up and the collar open.

I said, "Mr. Sprague, I'd like to talk to you in private."

"We're alone," he said.

I took out the Lynch ID and handed it across the desk. He

scanned it very quickly, nodding to himself as he did so. Then he snapped it shut and returned it to me. He stood up, a finger at his lips, and he walked in a half crouch to the door. He stood in the doorway, looking both ways like a well-schooled child at a traffic intersection. Then he cocked an ear—I have heard this expression, but I never before saw anyone do it. He cocked an ear, and listened, and then he closed the door and came back to where I was standing.

"Mr. Sprague," I said, "I'm giving you the opportunity to serve your nation and the cause of freedom."

TWELVE

I Spent Close to an hour in Sioux Falls and broke my own record driving back to Sprayhorn. A cop flagged me down outside of Oak Bend but my Agency ID changed his mind. He offered me a police escort. I told him I didn't want to attract attention. He went back to his car and I went back to Sprayhorn.

The Chrysler was gone when I reached the motel. I went to my room and packed everything. I put my suitcases in the trunk of the car and gave the inside of the room a fast fingerprint wipe. There seemed little chance that they would fail to identify Richard John Lynch as Paul Kavanagh, but I saw no point in making it easier for them. If O'Gara's snap of my ID got lost, and if I managed to wipe up my office before I left, I had a chance of staying covered.

When Dattner returned I told him I wanted a gun. "A cop stopped me," I told him. "The ID changed his mind, but suppose he decided to take me in anyway? Give me something heavy. I want to knock down anything I wing."

I picked out a .44 Magnum that was guaranteed to stop an

elk. He had a spare shoulder rig, and I adjusted it over my uniform jacket and under my overcoat.

I told him about Sprague.

"Can he get men?"

"Four of them."

"They might talk."

"No. He's not telling them what it's all about. He says they're politically reliable anyway, though what that means to him is anybody's guess. But he won't tell them what he wants them for until he's got them rounded up and ready to play, and after that they won't have any chance to talk. He's got a good sense of theater for a trucker."

"He sounds like a good man."

"He's gung ho, if that's what you mean. He'd lead a charge up San Juan Hill if I told him to, but I think he's an idiot. He has no idea what's going on. For all he knows I'm Mao Tse-tung's brother-in-law."

"You no look Chinese."

"I don't think it would matter to him if I did."

"Maybe not. Get any signs?"

I opened the back door and hauled out a metal frame with a rectangular sign that said MEN WORKING. "The best I could do," I said. "How did you do?"

"Pretty good." He hoisted his sign, carried it over to the Chrysler. He opened the trunk, and I looked at two small sawhorses and a couple of detour signs. There were several little black smudge pots, too. "I had to get rid of the spare and the jack to make room," he said. "Left them both on the side of the road, and all I could think of was what would I do if I had a flat. The answer was I would stop the next car and shoot somebody, but at this hour on these roads you can wait for hours for the next car." He took out his pills and swallowed two of them. He offered them to me but I shook my head.

"You've got to stay alert," he said.

"I'm all right. You're eating those like candy."

"Don't worry about me."

"You can get excessively hopped up on those, can't you? I

mean to the point where they get in your way."

"Don't worry about me. I've used them before, I know how they work."

"All right."

"They beat falling asleep, I'll tell you that."

"All right."

Maybe the reason I didn't want the benzedrine was that I felt as though I was already on it. There was the same utter absence of fatigue, the same ability to concentrate intensely upon one thing at a time, the same jittery feeling that was not so much nervousness as the sensation of moving at a faster speed than the rest of the world. This was probably caused by a number of things, adrenalin not the least of them, but the effect was the same as if one of my endocrine glands was secreting amphetamines into my bloodstream. My last night's sleep had been brief, and too many hours had passed since then, but even so nothing like fatigue ever hit me. Even on the endless ride back from Sioux Falls I had stayed on top of things.

There was one bad time, not exhaustion but a sort of misdirection of attention. It came along between the time when George drove away in the Chrysler and my own departure for the base. For a few minutes I had little to think about and less to do, and I made the mistake of letting my mind wander.

This had one good effect—I thought of a possible future hangup and figured out how to handle it if it came up—but it also eventually led me away from the entire operation. I started thinking about the future, not the future of the job but the *future* future.

I thought about my island. I should have known right away that something was wrong, because the island and the job had nothing to do with each other and didn't belong in the same day's thinking. And I thought about certain things I might do with my million dollars. I would have to buy the island, of course, and I would have to set up some sort of system to pay the taxes on it through a third party. And I might want to make certain improvements on the island. Water, for example. Maybe there was a way I could pipe in fresh water without drastically altering the present arrangement.

There was also the hurricane threat. The hurricane season wasn't far off, and the Keys were usually hit hard, and any strong wind would tear the living hell out of my shack. If I could put up the same sort of structure with concrete block instead of timber, it might make the difference between living through a hurricane or getting spattered all over the Gulf of Mexico. Of course concrete block would be a radical departure, but maybe the improvement in safety justified it.

Things like that.

And then, before I knew it, I was thinking about Sharon. My first reaction was one of surprise that I had thought about her at all, and after that I tried to remember how long it had been since I had last thought about her. A long time, I decided, and I let that play around in my mind, and I worked variations on the idea of Sharon combining with the idea of my island, and I began having imaginary conversations with her, and—

And I just caught myself in time.

I started the engine and got the hell out of the motel lot. It was too early to go to the base, but I had to be somewhere doing something or I was in all sorts of trouble. I had to stop thinking of Sharon, or of anything else not related to what was happening at the moment. The future had a million million unknowns, some about which I might speculate and others which could never be foreguessed, and there were things I knew I would do and things I knew I would not do and things I had as yet no inkling of, and they could all get together in the gray limbo of tomorrow. I had enough worries handling today.

The night sentry knew me. I had gone to my office once before in the middle of a sleepless night, largely to determine what the drill was in the off hours but also to let the night man familiarize himself with me. I was lucky. He didn't get many visitors at that hour, and he remembered me, so I got in now without the static that had attended my earlier night visit. I parked my car and looked around to see if Bourke and O'Gara were on the job. Their car wasn't around. I showed myself to the guard at my building. He was new, and didn't know me, but neither did he challenge me. I went to my office and gave it a quick sweep for prints, then went outside and did the same for the car on the chance that I wouldn't use it again. It wasn't much of a chance, but I did seem to have time on my hands.

Back in the office, I dug the Walker paraphernalia from my money belt and emptied the rest of the Walker garbage from my wallet. I had the feeling that I might be burning a bridge, but I also had a hunch that this was my last shot at this particular bridge, so I started a fire in a green metal wastebasket and fed Major John NMI Walker to it a scrap at a time. I saved Walker's driver's license because Lynch didn't have one.

I looked at my watch. It said it was 4:55. I picked up my phone and got the operator and asked what time it was and was told it was 4:59. I corrected my watch and started wiping the surfaces I had touched since my last print-sweeping job.

D-Day, 5 A.M. H-Hour less ninety minutes.

No. H-Hour less, say, somewhere between one hundred ten and one hundred fifty minutes. The trucks might not roll on the dot at 6:30, and it would take them at least twenty minutes to reach the ambush location.

H-Hour less two hours, roughly.

In two hours George Dattner and I would have to stop four armored trucks and a two-door Ford sedan. We would have to do something about four drivers armed with handguns, four front-seat passengers armed with automatic rifles, four guards in the Amarillo truck toting M-14s, and two MI majors armed with God knew what.

I left my office and headed across to the warehouse. It was

snowing again, coming down fairly hard. It seemed as though this ought to be either good or bad for our side, but I couldn't figure out which, so I stopped thinking about it.

Bourke and O'Gara were already on the job. They didn't seem to be doing anything vital. Bourke was watching a supply sergeant issue ammunition to a group of enlisted men, while O'Gara was putting up a fair show of overseeing things in general.

It was O'Gara who noticed me. "What do you know? We didn't expect you for at least an hour. Wear that uniform long enough and you'll start acting like a soldier."

"And lie in bed all day waiting for reveille?" I shook my head. "I'm only awake because I never got to bed. I spent the whole night running around like some kind of a nut."

"They finally reached you?"

"They finally reached me. They decided telegrams were unsafe and they sent some idiot in a private plane. He had to land in Sioux Falls and called me from there."

"So?"

"So they told him to deliver the word in person, and orders are orders in our league, too. He was stuck in Sioux Falls, so the mountain had to go to Mohammed. I drove there."

That reminded Bourke of something that had happened to him once in London, and he killed a few minutes telling us about it. I don't remember what it was, but I don't think it could have been very exciting.

When he was done, O'Gara asked me where I stood.

"I go along," I said. "Our office seems to be taking this Texas bit more seriously than I thought. It sounds as though they have half the state roped off."

"Beautiful."

"Uh-huh. I go along, I stay out of your way but I make myself generally useful, whatever that means. My main function is liaison. They're keeping a line open for me, and whenever we stop to take a leak I call home."

"It's our job, but your people want to watch us do it."

I nodded. "That's about the size of it. I had no sleep and it's how far to Amarillo? Seven hundred miles?"

"If you're a crow," O'Gara said. "Our route, we figure closer to nine."

"What do you figure to average? Forty-five?"

"Forty-five, but I'd settle for an honest forty. Figure an ETA of four a.m. tomorrow. Twenty, twenty-two hours on the road."

I looked at him.

"If you want dexedrine—"

"I've got bennies, but there's a limit anyway. I wish to hell I'd slept last night." I hesitated. "If I didn't have to drive, it would not exactly break my heart."

"You'd rather not take your car?"

"That says it."

They looked at each other. "I'd ask you to come with us—"

"I'd accept."

"—but I don't know that I can, Dick. We'll bend regs if we can get away with it. In this case it would be a clear contravention of orders. It's supposed to be Phil and me in that car and nobody else, and we'd get called down. We could stretch a point if you were military, but you're not, and it's our ass if they find out."

"Would they have to find out?"

"No way to keep it from them. I'm afraid there's no choice."

Bourke nodded in agreement. "We could grab a kid and have him drive for you," he suggested. "Give you a chance to sleep as far as Omaha, say, and then you could drop the kid off and take over."

That was just what I didn't want. It would lengthen the odds by one more man. I pretended to think about it. "I'll tell you," I said, "it's the stretch after Omaha that I'm worried about. I'm all right now, I'm just worried that the bennies might give out on me sooner or later. Suppose I take the car myself, and if I'm beat when we hit Omaha I pick up a driver there.''

''Anyway you want it.''

We left it at that, and I was where I'd started, no better and no worse. I hadn't expected them to let me tag along in their car. George and I had figured that as the best possible break, and had allowed for it as a chance, but we weren't counting on it.

''Let's give the routine a once-over,'' I suggested. ''If there's time. I wasn't paying much attention yesterday to the original convoy set-up, you know, from here to Omaha.''

''That's the easy part.''

''I realize that, but I'd like to know the order of vehicles and whatever emergency procedure you've arranged. Are you last in line or do you follow the Amarillo car? Or is the Amarillo vehicle last anyway? And where do you want me to be?''

We went into an all-purpose office and they laid it out for me with pencil and paper. The Amarillo truck was to be placed last in line, so that their Ford could ride on its tail and bring up the rear all at the same time. Later, when they picked up other convoy vehicles and got rid of the other three trucks, the procedure would be changed. I could ride almost anywhere else in the procession I wanted, except that they did not want me in the lead, directly in front of the Amarillo truck, or between it and them.

''So I can be the caboose?''

They said I could. We went over a few other points, and then I had another idea.

''Suppose I ride in the Amarillo truck?''

''It only seats two, Dick.''

''I mean in the back,'' I said. ''You've got four men with M-14s, a fifth hand wouldn't hurt. I could sit and doze, and if anything came up there would be one more man with a gun.''

''No room,'' Bourke said. ''They're cramped with four.''

"Are you sure? I could curl up on top of a crate, as far as that goes."

It was over-ruled, which didn't surprise me. They pointed out that I wasn't authorized to ride in army transport. Besides that, any spare space belonged to the guards. I made the point that it might be a better idea to load the guards in Omaha, so that they would be fresh for the last leg of the trip. They had already thought of this and planned to switch guards at the Omaha stop. Then why, I wondered, have guards along at all on the first stage of the journey?

They exchanged a long look. "That's a point," O'Gara admitted. "You know how we got to it, of course. We decided on guards, then we decided on a fresh detail going south from Omaha, and now we're stuck with four clowns who'll be riding to Omaha for no real purpose."

"Why not bump them?"

"Oh, I don't know. They're up, they know the drill, they've been issued guns and ammo." A snort. "The army way. If we drop them now we'll get static from the Bald Windbag, you can bet on it. Don't tell those boys, but they're along for the ride because it's easier than dropping them at this point."

I worked at it a little, but I didn't want to push it too hard. The boys with the M-14s were the one element we hadn't counted on in our original calculations, and even with our modifications since then I couldn't discount them as a major source of trouble. Still, there was a limit to the amount of static I could raise over them. You don't win men's confidence by telling them to take the bullets out of their guns. Sooner or later they start wondering what your angle might be.

It had been worth a try, like riding with them or in the truck. But I hadn't expected it to work, and it hadn't, and the status remained quo.

By now Sprague's truck should have arrived on the scene. By now George was supposed to be in position, ready to put the ball in play.

If not—

Every once in a while the Army does something on time. It happens just often enough so that the possibility can never entirely be ruled out. This was one of those times. After a lot of backing and maneuvering in the yard, the four trucks lined up facing the main gate. I went to my car and started the engine, and I pulled into position and let the motor idle with the choke about halfway out. Phil Bourke pulled their Ford up alongside me. O'Gara was running around outside like a football coach, shouting last-minute instructions to the drivers.

He hurried back, called something to me that was lost in a sudden gust of wind. Then he was inside his car.

I looked at my watch. At 6:30, right on the dot, the lead truck lurched forward and passed through the gate.

And I heard O'Gara talking in the car beside me. "Camelback Leader to Control," he was saying. "Camelback Leader to Control. We're going where it's warm, you poor suffering bastards. Six hundred thirty hours, six three zero and away we go—"

A radio. He was talking on a radio.

We hadn't figured on a radio.

THIRTEEN

MY CAR CLEARED the main gate a dozen or so yards behind Bourke and O'Gara's Ford. I dropped a little farther to the rear, reached inside my coat and took out the Magnum. I put it on the seat beside me.

The snow had let up again, but it hardly mattered. There was a steady wind blowing across from the southwest, driving loose snow across the windshield. I was wearing gloves, thin leather driving gloves, and my hands kept a tight grip on the steering wheel.

A radio. We hadn't allowed for radio contact because there was no point in it. Evidently Bourke and O'Gara were in touch with someone at Fort Joshua Tree, and how long could that contact be maintained? Maybe fifty miles? Not even that in bad weather, I guessed, so where was the percentage in setting it up in the first place? I decided it sounded like an idea Gen. Baldwin Winden would have come up with, and they must have decided it couldn't hurt to humor the old bastard.

The hell it couldn't. I had planned on developing car trouble, running my own bus off the road and giving them a honk for help. When they came back to give a hand, I could take them out of the play.

But forget all that. If they saw me in distress they might stop, or they might get on the squawker and call back to the base for assistance, figuring I could catch up with them later. Once they did that, a car or two would set out after us from Joshua Tree.

No good.

There was a bad moment. All I could think was that we were rolling closer and closer to the intercept point, with the odometer ticking off tenths of a mile, and Plan A of Step One was washed out, and I had to come up with a new wrinkle, and my mind was frozen. I took both hands off the steering wheel and made fists of them, pounding idiotically at the wheel. The car swerved and brought me out of it, and I fought my way out of a skid and stayed on the road.

I leaned on the gas pedal a fraction, closing the gap between my car and the Ford in front of me. My right hand dropped to the Magnum. A slug in one of their rear tires would do it, I decided. It would take them off the road, and they might not realize it was a gunshot that had done it, might read it as a blowout, and the truck up in front might not pay any attention to their disability, and—

I held the heavy gun in my lap. I was maybe twenty-five yards behind Bourke and O'Gara, and I could cut that in half if I wanted. I might be able to plink a tire at that range—if it was standing still, if I had a sandbag to brace my arm on, if I had checked out the Magnum and knew whether it threw high or low, right or left, and if there was no wind blowing.

As things stood, I'd be lucky to hit their car, let alone their tire.

I put the gun back on the seat. I checked the odometer. We were a hot mile and seven-tenths from the last access road before the intercept point. Their car had to be stopped as soon as possible after it crossed that intersection.

I moved to within twenty yards of them. The motorcade was holding a steady speed of forty-two miles an hour, good time for that sort of road. My eyes flitted from the car ahead to the odometer to the landmarks at the side of the road.

We reached the last access road. About fifty yards down, on the right, I saw George's Chrysler parked at the side of the road. His lights flashed twice as I crossed the intersection. All systems were go, everything was in motion.

I leaned on the horn and put the accelerator pedal on the floor.

The car shot forward, came up hard on the Ford ahead. I swung around to the left, pulled up almost even with them. Bourke was motioning for me to fall back in line. I had trouble keeping my hand off the gun beside me, but instead I held onto the wheel with my left hand and leaned across the seat toward him, pointing frantically at the rear of his car.

"Your tire!" I yelled.

He put a cupped hand to his ear. I pointed again and yelled in slow motion so that he could read my lips. Then I dropped my hand to grip the gun. If he didn't stop now—

The Ford slowed, pulled to the side of the road. I braked to a stop alongside it. I leaned across the seat, rolled down the window.

"Your left rear wheel," I said. "It's coming off."

"Something wrong with the tire?"

"No, the wheel." I had my hand wrapped around the Magnum now, holding it out of sight. "It's wobbling like a three-day drunk. It just started a few minutes ago and it looks as though it'll come off any minute."

O'Gara was out of the car, motioning at the truck ahead to keep on going. I don't think they even knew he'd stopped. Bourke picked up the radio and called in, trying to raise Control. I got out of the car on the driver's side, wedged the Magnum into the shoulder rig. I walked around the car with O'Gara to look at the wheel.

"Those idiots at Motor Pool were supposed to go over her top to bottom," he said.

"They must have left some bolts loose."

"Damned fools."

Bourke popped out on his side and came around. "They're sending a truck," he said.

"You called in?"

"Right. They're sending a repair crew. I suppose we'll catch them but this is crazy."

I put my hand inside my coat. O'Gara was bending over the wheel, his hands gripping the snow tire. Bourke stood alongside him. He was saying something about it having been a good thing that I noticed the trouble right away. I was trying not to listen to him, or to think of anything at all.

O'Gara never knew what happened. I drew the gun and fired in one liquid motion and the bullet entered his head alongside the left ear. I swung the gun around to Bourke. He was frozen. His face didn't even register changes of expression, and I felt that I could have held the pose for ten minutes and he never would have moved.

A moot point. The sound of the first shot was still echoing in the empty air when I squeezed the trigger a second time. It was easier than shooting out a tire on a moving car. He was a stationary target just five feet away from me, and the big slug tore half his head off.

Seconds later I was on their radio. I raised the pitch of my voice and came as close as I could to O'Gara's Boston inflection. "Camelback Leader to Control," I snapped. "Camelback Leader to Control. Hold that truck. Repeat, hold that truck. False alarm, snow on the wheel. Repeat, false alarm, hold the truck. Confirmation, please.--

The truck had already been ordered out. They called the main gate in time and the sentry caught it and ordered it back.

I left my own car in the road and drove on ahead in the Army Ford.

It took less than a minute to catch the rest of the convoy. They were lined up in the road with their engines off like circus elephants waiting for their cue. I passed the four of them on the left and pulled to a stop at the barricade.

A good job. Sprague's truck, a huge gray van with his name on the side, was stretched diagonally across the road. Alongside it was a convertible that looked as though it had collided with the van. There was actually nothing much wrong with the convertible. George had stolen it earlier, and some of Sprague's men had helped him kick in its fenders and turn it over onto its side.

I got out of the Ford. A few soldiers were milling around the overturned car waiting for someone to tell them what to do. The rest remained in the cabs of their trucks. The four guards in the Amarillo truck were nowhere in sight. I walked down the line.

"Everybody out," I called. "On the double, everybody out!"

The cab emptied. The soldiers left their guns in the cabs and piled out yawning. Someone asked what had happened to the other officers, and I said they had run into mechanical trouble down the road.

"Where the hell is everybody?" I demanded. "Somebody drove this car, some idiot must have been in the truck—"

A few soldiers went to check. "No one here, sir."

"Ambulance must have picked them up," I said. "And then they left this mess for us."

A soldier suggested he might be able to get the trucks around the car and van on the left. I glared at him. "Through that snow, solider? Are you serious?"

"I think there's room, sir."

"Remember what you're carrying, soldier. It's bad enough to be on a road like this. With this sort of cargo, you can damned well bet we stay on the road."

"Yes, sir," he said. *Yes, sir, you damned fool of an officer* is what he meant. But he wouldn't give it voice in a million years. Major John NMI Walker might be dead, but his uniform still commanded respect.

"We have to move the car," I said. "Then we can get the truck started and run it off the road. Where are the four boys from the Amarillo truck?"

"They refused to leave their post sir."

"Tell 'em to get the hell out here!"

Two men mumbled together. One, a PFC, spoke up.

"They said they were under orders to remain at their post, sir."

I scanned the road to the rear. George was approaching in my car. By now the detour signs were all posted, the road sealed in front of us and to our rear. I started for the Amarillo truck. Would they refuse to obey a direct order?

They might, I decided. And they might tip, and I might have four M-14s pointed at me.

"Well, those are their orders," I said, reconsidering. "How many of us are there? Eight of you men, is that right? Maybe we can do it without them. You, Corporal, get on that side, and—"

I posted them around the convertible, then slipped around it myself so that I was standing by the rear of the van.

"Everybody get a grip," I said. "We'll try to put her right side up so she can roll. Lift on three."

I knocked sharply on the back of the van. A bolt snicked back.

"One. Two."

The tailgate of the van dropped.

"And freeze," I said. "Not a sound. Nobody move."

They looked up, shocked. They saw me with the Magnum in my fist, and, behind me, Sprague and his boys, guns in their hands, piling out of the back of the van.

"That's right," I said. "You boys just hold onto the car, you won't get in trouble that way." To Sprague I said, "Good work, citizen. Keep them covered, no talk and no shooting. It's not over yet."

I headed back toward the Amarillo truck. I stopped on the way when George pulled up next to me. I told him about the crew with the M-14s. He nodded shortly, followed me to the truck.

There was a peephole in the back of the truck. It was at eye-level if you happened to be standing inside the truck. I was on the ground, so it was a couple of feet over my head. I stood too close to the truck to be seen and ordered the men out.

"We were told not to move, sir. No matter what."

"This is Major Walker talking," I said. "We've run into an overturned car and we need more men to get it out of the way."

"We were told—"

My stupid mistake; I was an officer reasoning with an enlisted man. That wasn't according to book. I said, "Who am I talking to, soldier?"

"Sergeant Lewis Flint, sir."

"Sergeant Flint, I order you to pile out on the double. That's a direct order, Sergeant."

There was a moment of silence. I glanced over at the convertible. The eight soldiers were in place. Sprague and his men had them well covered.

Then Flint said, "Sir, begging your pardon, sir, but we were instructed to disregard all future orders until arrival in Omaha. Begging your pardon, sir—"

I started to say something but George had a hand on my arm. I turned to him. He had a tin can in his hand. It was about five inches long and an inch in diameter and looked like a container for butane lighter fuel. He whispered to me to give him a hand up.

I locked my hands. He put one foot in the stirrups, hopped up, caught hold of the peephole with one hand. With the other hand he held the can to the opening. There was a hiss for ten seconds, a couple of muffled coughs, then silence.

He hopped down, shoved the can into a pocket. "We open that truck last," he said. "Leave the doors closed for the next ten minutes, then open 'em and get out of the way. Let it air for another ten minutes before anybody goes in to unload."

"What was it?"

"A kind of nerve gas. Lightning in closed quarters, but it disperses radidly in open air."

"I didn't know you had anything like that."

He grinned. "I'm full of surprises. That was nice shooting back there. I was afraid you might be rusty, but that was pin-point plinking. How come the change in procedure?"

"I told him about their radio. "We'd better keep it moving," he said. "They may have been scheduled to call in periodically. I love your man Sprague, incidentally."

"What did you tell him?"

"I kept it vague. As far as he's concerned, you're in command. I'm an errand boy. So I didn't want to get in your way."

"Fine."

We stopped at George's car. He had the Thompson assembled on the back seat. He brought it out, and we went on to where the patriots were guarding the soldiers. I said, "Mr. Sprague, citizens. You've met my colleague, Mr. Gunderson?"

They had.

"Good. The operation's running smoothly but time is short. Mr. Gunderson will take charge of our prisoners." George waved the Thompson at them and marched them off to the rear. "They won't be hurt," I told Sprague. "They're good American boys. It's not their fault that they're dupes, pawns in a leftist conspiracy. We'll have to put them out of action for a few hours. We already used gas to knock out four guards. It will wear off before too long, but for the time being they're dead to the world."

Sprague grunted. His four helpers were all considerably younger than he, tall rangy men in their middle and late twenties. They wore dungarees and heavy soled boots and jackets with sheepskin linings. One of them went in for sideburns in a big way. Otherwise they were clean-cut types.

"Let's get with it," I said. "Time's short."

Sprague got into the cab of his van. He started the engine, put the huge truck in reverse and eased the upset convertible off the road and into a drift of snow. One of his helpers got into the lead army truck and maneuvered it carefully around, positioning it back to back with the van. He dropped both tailgates, and the rest of the men swung into action, lifting the heavy crates one by one, carrying them out of the truck and across the tailgate bridge and stacking them in the van.

I looked at my watch. It was 7:06.

When I looked again it was 7:19 and I was opening the back of the Amarillo truck. I dropped the tailgate and got the hell out of the way, my hand over my face. There are dozens of different kinds of nerve gases and they all work in different ways. Some hit the respiratory system and kill you if you breathe them in. Others work through the skin; one drop on the back of the hand is enough to put you away. I didn't know what kind this was or how it worked or how long it remained effective, so I got out of the way fast.

At 7:30 I climbed into the truck. The M-14s I had worried about lay on the floor. They had never been fired. The men who would have fired them were also on the floor of the truck, their arms and legs at grotesque angles. Their faces were blue, which meant that the gas had probably been one of the respiratory types. I couldn't imagine anyone believing that they were only sleeping, so I carried them one at a time out of the truck and over to the side of the road. I stripped off their field jackets. They would never feel the cold, and Sprague's men would need them later on.

I went back to the truck for the M-14s. I scooped up the four automatic rifles. The M-14 was a weapon I knew well, and for all the bitching we had done about it, there were plenty of combat situations where nothing else could come close. There was a newer weapon in use overseas now, and the scuttlebutt had it that they jammed in action. We had said the same thing about the M-14 at first, I remembered.

I held one of the rifles in both hands, and for an odd minute I was back in Laos, and then the moment was gone before I could analyze it. I wondered if I could still take the thing apart and put it back together in the required time span, and then I wondered how important that sort of talent was nowadays, and then I turned the thoughts off and went to watch the loading operation.

They could never have worked as well when they were getting paid by the hour. One truck after another was maneuvered into position and its contents systematically transferred to the cavernous van. The crates were marked in code, so I could only guess at the scientific marvels they contained. Gas grenades, botulism cultures, nuclear mortar shells, all the rest. Science marches on, and man's reach keeps exceeding his grasp. I wondered how many varieties of nerve gas the van held. Properly deployed, I thought, the contents of Sprague's van could probably wipe out most of the country. Of course no one could use it all that efficiently—

They finished the third truck, backed it out and away. The kid with the sideburns swung the Amarillo truck around and brought it into position. Everybody got into the act, and I got out of the way and went over to see how George was doing.

He had them sitting down in the snow, eight of them. He was on his haunches facing them, with the submachine gun on his knees. He asked how it was going. I told him they had already cracked the last truck.

"The guards?"

"I moved them on over to the other side."

"How are they?"

"Still unconscious," I said.

"Good." He grinned. "How does it feel to be back in action?"

"It doesn't feel."

"Huh?"

I told him to forget it. One of the men was raising his hand. It was the PFC who had wanted to try running the trucks across the field. I thought for a minute that he wanted to go to the toilet.

George asked him what he wanted.

"I want to get out of here alive," he said.

"You will."

"I don't want to be a hero, sir." He paused for a moment, as if wondering whether or not he was supposed to call us *sir*. "None of us, uh, want to be heroes. I don't know what this is all about, sir, and I, uh, don't want to know. That's all, sir."

He was very young. I looked at the rest of them and realized that they were all very young. The four hardnoses in the Amarillo truck had been older. This figured—if you were picking a man to start blasting with an automatic rifle, you chose someone whose experience wasn't limited to the target range. But any clown could sit in a truck.

"Just do as you're told," I told him. I looked around at the rest of them. "You'll all get out of this alive."

They digested this. Then another one had a question, and George nodded at him. I suppose it made sense to keep them talking, I don't know.

"Sir, what Major Walker said before. About us being dupes?"

Oh, they were that, all right.

"In a Commie conspiracy. I don't know what it's all about, but I suppose Majors Bourke and O'Hara were Red agents? Who infiltrated the military? And planned to ship the cargo to subversives?"

He got O'Gara's name wrong, but the rest sounded good enough. Give a man paper and pencil and he'll write out your lie for you and believe it when you read it back to him.

I let George pick it up. "Good thinking, soldier," he said. "You've got the right idea, but I'm afraid it's more complicated than you think—"

I stood up. He didn't need me there, and I didn't want to hear the rest of it. I got the radio from the Ford and put through a call to Central. The clown on the other end said he'd been trying to reach me, so maybe it was just as well that I had called.

I said, "Camelback Leader to Control. Camelback Leader to Control. I cannot read you. Repeat, I cannot read you. Over."

He came back loud and clear.

After a minute I said, "Camelback Leader to Control, I've got your signal but you're not clear. Repeat, I've *blip gurgle* but you're not *gurgle gurgle snap*. Please *grunt gurgle*. Over."

He came back again, and I cut in on him. "Control, this is Camelback Leader. We're losing reception all *gurgle* place.

We're on schedule and everything's fine but this *gurgle* radio. Too much weather. We'll *gurgle snap gurgle gurgle click.*"

I smashed the set with the butt of the Magnum. They weren't going to hear from us again, and now they could blame it on the snow.

When the loading operation was finished I had Sprague get his men together. They had worked up a good sweat, and Sprague himself was puffing hard. But the work hadn't undercut their enthusiasm. They were as bright-eyed as when they started.

"You men have done good work," I said. "I want to congratulate you. When a country has the support of men like you—"

I felt as though I was laying it on a little thick, but once I had set the tone it was hard to let go. I shook hands with them in turn, and they told me their names, and I mumbled heroic words of encouragement.

"We're halfway home now," I went on. "As you all know, the command at Fort Joshua Tree has been completely riddled by Communists and pink sympathizers. Mr. Gunderson and I have to get this van out of sight before they start sending out aerial recon teams. More important, we've got to put the truck convoy back on the road. A helicopter can't tell whether the trucks are full or empty, or whether the men driving them are soldiers or citizens." I pointed to the pile of field jackets taken from the dead guards. "Try those on," I said. "See how they fit."

The four helpers managed to get into the four available jackets. Sprague was left out. I took off my own overcoat and gave it to him. "You'll take the convoy car," I told him. "Wear this, and take the last spot in line."

The coat was tight on him, but he managed to get into it. I took his jacket in return. It must have looked ridiculous over my uniform, but I didn't much care.

I said, "Your destination is Omaha." I briefed them on the

route and told them to make no stops en route. "You're behind schedule, so try to make up the time as well as you can. Don't go over sixty, but maintain as close to that speed as you can without pushing it. When you get to Omaha, split up immediately. Park the trucks on side streets, leave the jackets in them, and head for home."

"Won't they get suspicious when the trucks don't reach the Omaha destination?"

"Right. But by then we'll have the van a long ways from here. We're buying time, that's all."

"Check."

"If you're stopped on the road, refuse to answer questions. Don't tell them a thing. No matter who interrogates you, no matter what kind of credentials you're shown. Follow?" They nodded. "There are a lot of Commie types in positions of authority, and a lot of good Americans who'll go along with them because they don't know any better. Just clam up." I thought for a moment. "Don't even reveal your names," I went on. "Are you carrying any identification? Wallets, licenses?"

I waited while they went through their pockets and handed me things. I took the money from their wallets and returned it to them. "We'll return the rest later," I said. "And here—" I took out my wallet, counted out five hundred dollars each for them— "for expenses. You'll receive further recognition of our gratitude several weeks from now."

To a man, they denied any desire for compensation. But to a man they took the five hundred.

"Now, Mr. Sprague. I'm afraid you may never see your truck again, citizen."

He returned my smile. "Sort of suspected as much," he said. "Don't be worrying about her, she's insured."

"Don't report the loss. We'll be in touch with you and you'll be reimbursed in cash."

"Fair enough."

I couldn't think of anything else. I cleared out the Bourke-O'Gara Ford, took the suitcases from the trunk and the radio from the front seat, grabbed up some papers from the glove compartment. Sprague pulled the van over to the side of the road to make room for the convoy. Then he got in the Ford, and the rest of the men climbed into the cabs of the trucks and got the engines going.

George called me over. His captives seemed completely at ease. He took out a tube of pills and gave it to me. "For the drivers," he said. "One apiece, now. To prevent fatigue."

"Bennies?"

"Not exactly," he said. "Make sure they take 'em."

I went from the truck to truck passing out the pills. "Take it now," I told each man. "Swallow it down. It's a guarantee against tiring for the next twelve hours. Even if you're not tired, take it. You might be interrogated, and they might use some truth serum on you. This makes you immune to it, with no harmful side effects."

They all took their pills. One of them had trouble getting his down without water, but he made it. Another, the one with the sideburns, wanted to know if I had anything to help him withstand torture. I told him the pill would also raise his pain threshold. This reassured him, and he swallowed it.

Sprague gave me some last-minute instructions on operating the truck. How to handle weigh-in stations, where to tank up, that sort of thing. I thanked him again for his cooperation. He quoted me the fair market value of the truck. I don't recall the figure, but it seemed like an honest estimate. I told him he'd be reimbursed for the same truck in new condition. He said that wasn't necessary, and I told him it was standard. "The way the Government gives away money, some of it might as well go to the right kind of people." He allowed as how he couldn't argue with that.

I gave the sign, and the first truck dropped into gear and took off. I remembered something and called the driver down. "Don't forget the road block up ahead," I said. "Take it down, then have the last man put it up again when you're through."

I suppose he would have figured this out for himself. But

he just nodded and said he would, and I waved him on again, and off they went, four khaki trucks in a row, with Sprague bringing up the rear.

The noise of their engines faded. Then the wind died down and I heard them again. I went over to George. He had a strange look on his face and he avoided my eyes. "Something I want to check," he said. "Hold onto this for me."

He handed me the Thompson. I told the men to remain seated and walked off after him. "It's silly to argue about it," he said levelly. "I could do it, sure, but it's not my kind of thing. We're running late, Paul. Now if you want to make a case out of it—"

He saw my face and he shut up.

I said, "Wait for the question before you come up with the answer. I want the M-14, that's all."

"Oh."

"I never used one of these. I want something I'm checked out on, like an M-14."

I picked one off the pile and left the Thompson in its place. George said, "I'll never figure you. Never."

"Then why try?"

I went back to the eight soldiers. Their line had been reshaped into a flat semicircle and they were talking about women. They barely raised their eyes at my approach. I wondered if any of them had laid Col. Carr's wife and if they had enjoyed it more than I did.

Sometimes in Cambodia we went out on three and four man patrols. Sometimes we took prisoners, and on patrols like that you can't take prisoners. They wouldn't approve in Geneva. So we don't tell them.

The M-14 was an old friend. *Ratatatatatatatat*. It was all over before the barrel was more than slightly warm to the touch.

I turned and saw George. You prick, I thought. He couldn't do it, but he had to watch.

FOURTEEN

AT 12:04 GEORGE SAID, "It's official, old buddy. We're criminals."

I was dozing, a shapeless half dream that fled from memory when I opened my eyes. The truck radio was playing country music. I thought he must have heard a news flash and asked him what it was all about.

"Not that," he said. "No, there hasn't been anything. We just crossed a state line, that's all."

"Oh."

"We're in Minnesota. That makes us federal offenders. They can put the FBI on our tail, and then there'll be no way out."

"Funny."

He looked at me. "Something wrong? I don't expect big laughs, but you don't have to get surly."

"I'm half asleep, that's all. Give me a minute."

"Sure."

I rubbed my eyes, straightened up in the seat beside him. I checked my watch and announced the time. "They must be in Omaha by now," I said.

"Maybe."

"Or close to it. Where are we?"

He pointed to a map. I picked it up. "The next town we hit is Canby," he said. "Can you find it?"

I found it, a dot on the map just east of the South Dakota state line and almost due west of Minneapolis and St. Paul.

"Where do we stop?"

"I told you."

"Tell me again."

"The closest town is Good Thunder. I don't know if it's on that map. Middle of the state, southern tier. Look for Mankato and then—"

"Got it."

"It's south of Mankato and—"

"I found Good Thunder. Where do they get these names?"

"It's an Indian word, it means Lakanookee. You know, it's just about impossible to get a laugh out of you, Paul. The barn's on a county road southwest of Good Thunder. One of our agents grew up on the farm, inherited it a couple of years ago when his mother died. Ever since I met him he talked about retiring there some day."

"I hope he waits a few days."

"I think he's dead, matter of fact. He was in Barcelona and he disappeared. When they disappear in friendly countries we don't usually see them again."

"Maybe he's on his farm, waiting for us."

"Maybe the whole farm disappeared in a flash flood. That's one thing we never prepared for."

"Flash floods?"

"Mmmm."

"May that be our greatest worry."

I sat back and watched the road. I asked him if he wanted me to drive. He said he was doing fine, and I didn't press it. The road was narrow and curvy, the snow was heavy, and the rig would have been a pain to drive on a turnpike in July as far as I was concerned.

A few miles down the line I said, "George?" He grunted. "What were those pills?"

"What pills?"

"The pep tonic for Paul Revere and the Raiders."

"Who?"

"Sprague."

"Oh," he said. He chuckled, and he didn't say anything, so neither did I. Then he asked me what I thought they were.

"I didn't think about it at the time. If they were really bennies I suppose you would have had me tell them they were Spanish Fly. What do they do, induce amnesia?"

"In a sense."

"Oh."

He had that smile on his face. He said, "Time-delay capsules The coating dissolves in two to three hours, depending upon the acidity of the stomach and the amount of change in your pocket. Then instant bliss."

I didn't say anything.

"Little black pills." He glanced at me. "I told you I had a few surprises. You must have guessed."

"I suppose so."

"The usual diagnosis is heart failure. A good autopsy within forty-eight hours will show more, but in this case it doesn't really matter, does it?"

"No."

"I get the feeling it bothers you."

I shook my head. "No. Why should it?"

"Good point."

A few miles later he said, "They would have talked, Paul."

"No question about it. Not much they could have said, though. And if they got away in Omaha, then I'm not so sure they would have talked. Especially once they found out they'd been conned. They'd have kept their mouths shut forever."

"What are the odds on all five of them getting clear in Omaha?"

"Long odds. Not much they could tell anybody."

"They can describe you."

"General Windy can do it better."

"They can describe me, too. And pick out my photo, if it comes to that. Once they're identified the truck becomes hot. That's the only problem, right? We'll have it cured before anybody identifies them or figures out that Sprague had a truck. From then on the identification works in our favor. What'll you bet that at least two of the five are in the Klan? Or some other right-wing thing? That fits the Texas story, drags one more red herring across the road."

"True."

"You don't sound convinced, Paul."

"No, you're right," I assured him. "Anyway, it doesn't matter. It's over four hours now, they're all dead. Unless—"

He looked at me. "Unless what? You saw them take the pills, didn't you?

"Oh, sure. But say one of them threw up before the pill worked. Or had diarrhea and somehow flushed the pill before zero hour. And then he'd see the other men dropping like flies and he might want to tell somebody about it. Or say one pill just took a lot longer to dissolve, and the one left alive figured things out. You remember that movie with Edmund O'Brien? *D.O.A.* or something, he's been fatally poisoned at the opening but he manages to get to the cops before he goes? I saw it years ago, I—"

"Oh, Christ."

"Probably nothing to worry about, George."

"You son of a bitch. You're sitting there and smiling, you son of a bitch."

"Well, you know," I said. "I wouldn't want you getting over-confident, George. Got to keep you honed to a keen edge."

He let it hang there for a while. Then he laughed, but it sounded as though he was pushing it.

We were on the road ourselves not long after the truck

convoy pulled out. The few things that had to be done beforehand were worth the time they took. Sooner or later someone was going to know something was wrong, and sooner or later a team from Fort Tree would check the route and find out what had happened and where. The idea was to make all this occur later instead of sooner.

We brought the stolen Chrysler back into the intercept area. It was clean, so we didn't mind abandoning it, but it was an attention-getter, and this way it would be out of sight until the team from Fort Tree came down. We left all our road signs in place to insure that. Accidental discovery by some citizen would cut our lead time to the bone, and the road signs would keep most citizens off that stretch of road and might coax any others into interpreting anything they saw as an accident the authorities already knew about.

The bodies were easy. We had the snow to thank for that. George had already tucked our two majors into a drift, and when I went back to check out their pockets it was hard to find them, the snow had erased all traces. I decided it wasn't worth digging them up and left them there.

We gave the other twelve the same treatment. We hauled them far enough from the road so that they would have been tough enough to spot even without the snow, and then piled white stuff on them. We left tracks in the snow, of course, but the wind figured to wipe them out within half an hour.

There were a lot of extra guns around—handguns returned to us by Sprague's men, the M-14s, the Thompson, a few stray rifles. They went in the back of the van—"A dividend for our *compañeros*," George called them. I figured it was quicker than burying them.

The van also got all of the garbage from the army Ford, plus my own luggage. Some of it would have to be destroyed, but we could paw through it at our leisure.

We left the crippled convertible at the side of the road. It was clean, like the Chrysler. My own rental car bothered me a little. I had cleaned it out, but it would trace to John NMI Walker, who in turn would trace to Lynch. They were going to guess Lynch anyway, so it didn't really make a hell of a difference. Still, it bothered me; I told George we should have put it on one side of the empty trucks and he told me I was building a case out of nothing.

"Slam it into the convertible," he suggested. "Make it look good."

"Make what look good?"

"The accident, the reason why the road is closed. Hell, I don't care. Dig a hole and bury it. Fold it up and put it in your pocket. Take it and shove—"

I got in the Chevy and drove it a nice steady twelve miles an hour into the upset convertible. Thinking back, I suppose the main reason I did this was because it's the sort of thing everybody secretly wants to do. I was braced for the impact, of course, and I stopped accelerating instinctively a few instants before the collision, and twelve miles an hour is not all that fast, but it was still a hell of a sensation. And it did more damage to both cars than I had expected.

When I got out of the car George told me it looked like fun.

"It was," I admitted. "If you want to try it, the Chrysler's just down the road. You can make it a spectacular three-car smashup."

For a moment I thought he was going to try it. Then he said, "Oh, the hell with it, it's a waste of time. What did we forget?"

"Sprague's jackets."

They went in the van. So did the wallets we had taken from the five men. If there was anything else, we didn't have the time to stand around figuring it out. We got in the cab, and George started it up and stalled it twice figuring out where the gears were. Once he got the hang of it, though, he wasn't bad at all.

The radio announced said we were listening to the Twin Cities' home of countrypolitan music. He said this right after a newscast during which he had said nothing at all concerning our operation. This didn't mean anything one way or the other. Whatever happened, it didn't figure to make the papers. "Three months from now there might be a paragraph in Drew Pearson's column," George had said, "and then someone important will tell him please to write about something else, and he'll expose a highway construction scandal. That's all."

The radio played something with too many guitars. George slowed the truck, killed the radio, and said we were here. At first I thought he was crazy. Then I saw that there was a space ten yards wide between two fences and that there were no trees in the space. That was the only indication that it was a road.

"There's two feet of snow there," I said.

"We'll make it. I'll back it in."

We kept getting stuck and he kept rocking us loose and we were in the barn sooner than I'd have guessed possible. Partly in the barn, anyway; the cab and half of the rest remained uncovered. I was going to point this out to George, but he answered ahead of time. "No neighbors anywhere near here, and we can't be seen from the road. C'mon."

"What now?"

"Grab a broom. We've got a hundred yards of tracks to cover."

There were brooms in the barn. We each took one and waded out to the road, walking in our own tire tracks. Then we backtracked all the way, using the brooms to fill the tracks with snow. The top ten inches of snow were loose and powdery, which made it easier. A wind would have been extra help. For the time being, though, we had to live without one.

It took a lot of time. Walking backwards, filling in tire tracks with a broom. A hundred yards, after all, was a substantial distance. It was approximately the length of my island, but it was a lot easier to walk the length of my island than to trudge backwards through snow, and—

I reminded myself not think about my island.

We quite before we'd done the whole hundred yards. It was fundamentally absurd to eliminate tracks all the way to the foot of the truck itself. Anyone close enough to see them would see the truck, too. We gave up twenty yards from it and went into the barn and set our brooms against the wall.

"Now we pray for snow," George said.

"But not too much. Or we won't get out."

"We'll get out," he said. "Think of all the *revolucionistas* who are counting on us. Pardon me. *Counterrevolucionistas.* Pardon me again, *contrarevolucionistas.*"

There was enough food for a week, but he assured me we'd be on our way within twenty-four hours. I said, *"Veinte y cuatro horas,"* and he winked. He asked me if anyone had thrown any Portuguese at me. No one had. He said I would have covered it anyway. I said we'd never know, and I for one would never care, and I was hungry.

There was bread, butter, four different kinds of luncheon meat, some cold chicken, twelve cans of beer (and a can opener; this impressed me). There was milk, Scotch whiskey, chocolate bars. Other things too that I don't remember.

I asked what was poisoned. He threw back his head and roared. "The Scotch," he said. "Whatever you do, stay away from the Scotch."

The son of a gun even had glasses. I poured each one half full of Scotch. He took his and asked what we should drink to.

I suggested brotherhood.

"The Brotherhood of Man?"

"Keep it simple," I said. "Just brotherhood."

"Fine. To brotherhood. How do you say that in Español?"

"You don't. To brotherhood."

I think he was waiting to see if I would drink mine before he drank his. I might have played the game, but by now I really did want that drink. I tossed it off, and he thought about playing games and decided it wasn't worth it, and drained his own glass.

FIFTEEN

WHEN WE FINISHED eating he lit a propane stove and rolled out a pair of army surplus sleeping bags. "All the comforts of home," he said. "I don't think you can see the stove from outside." I went outside, and he was right.

He thought we ought to sleep in shifts. I didn't, and said so. If they found us we couldn't possibly shoot our way out. He suggested that some tramp might stumble in.

"And murder us in our sleep? If you tried that on your computer it would laugh at you."

He thought it over. "Yeah, you're right," he said. "It's not worth the aggravation. The hell with it."

He took a sleeping pill. I didn't want one. I told him someday he would take a black pill by mistake. He told me, pleasantly, to go screw myself. I stripped to my underwear and got into the sleeping bag. There were a few dozen things I had to do, and I thought of about half of them before I fell asleep.

It must have been around five-thirty when we sacked out. I put in an honest eight hours. If I dreamed, I wasn't aware of it. I woke with the sudden thought that I had to go through

Bourke and O'Gara's luggage. There was that thought, instantaneous and undeniable, and then I was awake, and my watch said 3:42.

George was snoring gently. I let him sleep. I opened the back of the van, but it was too dark inside to see anything. I remembered seeing a flashlight hanging on the wall of the barn, and I walked to where I thought it might have been, and it was there. I couldn't have been more pleased with myself if I had just walked on water.

I climbed up into the truck. It wasn't snowing and didn't look as though it had snowed while I was asleep, but somewhere along the line we got the wind we'd hoped for. The driveway looked as though it hadn't seen a car or truck since the last Indian uprising.

I went through everything we'd thrown in the truck. The wallets, the suitcases, everything. For the most part, I didn't do more than establish that we had a lot of crud in the truck that deserved burning and/or burial. But I did find a baby camera in O'Gara's luggage, plus a roll of exposed film. He'd taken one shot of my ID that I knew of, and it was possible that it hadn't been processed yet. If that was so, then my prints never got to Washington.

As far as I knew, those prints were the only solid link between Richard John Lynch and me.

I don't know how long George might have slept. When it got to be six in the morning I decided that anything over twelve hours amounted to criminal self-indulgence. I shook him awake. "Get up," I said. "It's morning, I've got a dozen questions for you."

"In a while. Oh, God, I think I've got a barbiturate hangover. Let me eat something. I feel like hell."

We ate ham sandwiches and drank milk. He came slowly back to life. While he was doing this I took the garbage that had to be burned outside. I set a garbage can lid on top of the snow and built a little fire in it, feeding the stuff in a little at a time. It was mostly paper. After a few minutes he joined me and contributed a handful of paper. I fed it to the fire without looking at it.

"There's a well out in back," he said. "For the clothes and stuff. Get rid of that uniform. I've got trucker clothes in back, and keep a suit for afterward. Everything else goes."

"They'll look in the well."

"If they get here. The hell, let 'em. There's nothing traceable, is there?"

There wasn't, and it was impossible to dig in the frozen ground. We uncovered the well, threw a lot of clothing into it, and piled snow on top. Back in the barn, I started in on my questions.

"First of all, the route. Do we take the Mississippi Valley south or cut east first?"

"East. It's longer, but I feel better about it."

"All right. What kind of roads? Not turnpikes or main roads, obviously, but won't we be conspicuous on back roads?"

"We would. That's why we take the pikes." He unfolded a Shell map of the country that just showed major highways. "Straight east through Wisconsin, pick up the Wisconsin freeway south of Milwaukee. South on that, onto the Belt around Chicago. Then there's one stretch of turnpike through Illinois and Indiana and Ohio and on across Pennsylvania all the way to the coast. We don't go all the way, we pick up the Penn-Can and head south. It takes us—"

"How can we do that?"

"Easy. We take turns driving and—"

"There's a weighing station at every turnpike entrance. We have to show papers, we need all sorts of invoices and crud—"

"We've got them."

I looked at him. "You do your homework, don't you?"

"You betchum. Hang on, I'll show you."

He went to the back of the barn and returned with a manila

envelope. He spilled it out on the ground, and he had everything but a sweepstakes ticket. There were invoices and bills of lading and chauffeurs' licenses and membership cards in the International Brotherhood of Teamsters.

"See?" he said. "Turnpikes. They're fast and easy, and we are the Thornhill Hauling Corp. That's what it says on the registration and that's what it'll say on the truck once we paint her. I've got paint, I've got stencils. I've worked for my million, Paul. We get on that road and we stop for fuel and that's it. We stop for diesel fuel and change drivers. Period. We roll right on through, we swing along the coast to Orlando and cut west to Tampa and we're home. There's even a pretty good road from Orlando to Tampa. I checked, I know. See?"

"I'm impressed."

"Sometimes I even impress myself. What else?"

"You," I said. "What's your cover?"

"Me?"

"You. The last they heard of you was Monday morning when they sent you to Amarillo. You never got there and they never heard from you. You must have something. What?"

"I'm in Guatemala."

"Huh?"

He grinned. "You heard right. I called the office from Chicago Monday and begged out of Amarillo. I told them something hot was breaking and I had to go to Miami. I called in again from Pierre when I went to collect street signs. I told them I was in Miami and had to leave the country."

"Suppose they kept a record of the call?"

"No way to trace. They could have traced it at the time, but I know standard procedure and they wouldn't. I called into a line that just records messages for playback later."

"How does Guatemala fit in?"

"I go there when this is over. I have something to do there, as a matter of fact. It'll take two days, but I can make it look as though it took that many weeks. Then I come back from Guatemala, and I say I've been to Guatemala, and by God I have. I'll even have a souvenir for my secretary. Don't teach Grandma to suck eggs, Paul.''

We wiped the truck down and spray-painted the parts of the box with Sprague's markings on them. He had a battery-operated compressor to simplify things, and his paint was a close enough match for the van's body color so that we didn't have to do the whole thing. While the body dried we changed the color of the cab from red to green. Then we laid stencils on the sides of the box and labeled it *Thornhill*. We altered the state markings and added weight information to fit the papers we carried. Finally, we took off the South Dakota plates and substituted Illinois ones. The old plates went in the cab to be dumped in the first deep water we crossed. The stencils were cardboard. We burned them. The paints and brushes and the compressor were the sort of a thing a man might keep in a barn, so they stayed there.

We took the food along with us in the cab. He wanted to take along the Scotch and the beer, but I wouldn't let him. I pointed out that it was against the law. We left them in the barn, and left the can opener so that whoever found the beer wouldn't have to tear the tops off with his teeth. The sleeping bags we rolled up and left. George told me I ought to take the propane stove along, that it would come in handy on the island. I said I preferred fires in the open. He wanted to know what I did when it rained. I said I waited for it to stop, which it always did sooner or later, and I also said I didn't want to talk about the island.

We were on our way by early afternoon.

The trip was boring. It was the kind of trip that was supposed to be boring, and the only way it would have been exciting was if something had gone wrong. Nothing did, which was the general idea, but after a few hundred miles I found myself almost wishing for a crisis.

We started out with the radio going. Halfway through

Wisconsin neither of us could stand it any more. The newscasts were worst of all, because of course we listened to them intently, and of course there was nothing about us on them. The absence of publicity worked to our advantage, but it also worked on our nerves.

So I got edgy and kept changing stations, hoping to find one that would cease to irritate me, until George caught my mood and switched the thing off altogether. That left us alone with each other, which was worse, but I never even considered turning the damn thing on again, and I think if George had done so I would have shot him.

We tried talking, but that didn't work either, and by the time we hit the Illinois line the motif had been established. Silence, that was the word for the day.

George drove as far as the Wisconsin pike. We picked it up a little ways south and west of Milwaukee. It occurred to me that Sharon lived in Milwaukee and that I wasn't supposed to think about her. This might have been harder, but fortunately I took the wheel at that point and was able to think instead about driving. I had never driven anything that size before, and at first there was a lot of thinking involved.

There was also some tension, for a while, at turnpike entrances. But by the time we left Illinois and entered Indiana—with George driving again—I couldn't worry much about our cover slipping. The papers were in order, the weight was right, the truck was clean, and there was just no reason on earth for anyone to suspect otherwise.

We didn't even have to worry about a speeding ticket, because the speed limit was seventy and everybody was doing eighty and our truck couldn't make more than sixty-seven with a tail wind. It got so that it didn't much matter which of us was driving. When I drove I had my hands on the wheel and my foot on the gas pedal and my eyes on the road. When George drove I had both feet on the floor, my hands in my lap, and my eyes either closed or on the road, looking at the same view that was there in front of me ever since Chicago.

There was nothing to do but think, and most of the thoughts that came to mind concerned subjects I had already determined not to think about. I didn't want to review the past or muse about the future, and that left only the present, and the present was me and George and the truck. My mind couldn't do very much with the truck, so that left me and George.

I did a lot of thinking about both of us.

This went on for a long time. Sometimes it was day and sometimes it was night. Sometimes it snowed, but there was never much snow, and toward the end there was no snow on the ground, either.

Sometimes I dozed off, but not often, and I never dropped into anything more than a light dream state. George was eating pills again and, as far as I knew, never even closed his eyes.

And then, after close to eighteen hundred miles of driving and roughly thirty hours of endless tedium, George made a phone call.

It was eight at night, Thursday. We were in Georgia, we had been in Georgia for hours. The current road was a stretch of the Interstate Highway System with the services off the road. George took one of the exits and drove to a service station. The gauge showed almost half a tank, so I asked why.

"I want to call ahead."

"Fine."

"Want to tag along?"

"Why? You're a big boy, you know how to make a phone call. The dime does in the little slot in the middle. The big one's for quarters."

"Suit yourself."

He was gone about ten minutes. By the time he came out I had paid for the gas and moved the truck clear of the pumps. He got into the cab next to me. I looked at him, and he had an odd expression on his face. I tried to remember the last time I'd seen it.

"I called them," he said.

"And?"

"They were surprised. They hadn't heard a word, they didn't think we took it off. They can take delivery at 3:30 tomorrow afternoon in Tampa."

"What's that, three hundred miles? No problem."

He said, "They made a point of telling me to bring it straight in tonight. They know a warehouse where we can put the truck, and they'll give us beds for the night."

"Sounds good."

"You think so?"

"Why not?"

"I don't know." He sat silent, opened his mouth to say something, then clammed up again.

"What?"

"Something in his voice. We talked in Spanish and it's harder to read a voice in a foreign language. Know what I mean?"

I decided to let him do it himself.

"I'll tell you," he said when I didn't. "They might be thinking about a cross."

"So we'll go to Tampa and stay somewheres else."

"I thought of that. I don't know." His eyes caught mine, then dropped. He waited a beat, then straightened up with decision. "No," he said. "No, what it comes down to is I don't like Tampa. They want delivery at 3:30; that's when we show up at the pier. Tampa, the whole city is so full of so many people, I don't want to spend an extra minute in it. Where are we now? Is there a city around?"

I checked the map. "Waycross. Brunswick. Hmmm."

"Something substantial. Are we anywhere near Savannah?"

"Oh, so we are. It's closer than either of the others, actually. I missed it."

"Well, that's good. At least it sounds good to me. What do you think?"

"About what?"

"About spending the night in Savannah and hitting Tampa tomorrow. What did you think we were talking about?"

"Oh," I said. I took a breath. "I'm sorry, I think my mind is coming apart at the seams. I guess it sounds good. At this point you could tell me to go to Washington and I would do it. Where do you want to stay? I know Savannah, but I mean *where* in Savannah—"

He put a hand on my arm. "Easy," he said and started chuckling. "I knew I was in bad shape, but you're even more of a case. Let me drive. We could both do with ten hours in a real bed. Don't you worry, I'll find us something."

I wasn't worried.

What he found us was a tourist court that catered to long-haul truckers. There were three rigs already parked there, so we could forget about being conspicuous. He got us two cabins about twenty yards apart. We locked up the truck, and he went to his cabin and I went to mine.

I turned on the light, closed the door, locked it. I took off my trucker's clothes and hung them on a peg. I unstrapped my shoulder harness, took the gun out, and put the harness itself on the cabin's only chair.

I took a quick look through the window. George had already turned out his light.

The bed was a double. I took it down and put both pillows under the covers. I stepped back and decided they looked too white, so I wrapped the top one in the bedspread. I left the light on for ten minutes, then turned it off.

I carried the Magnum and stood behind the door in the darkness.

He waited an hour and twenty minutes. I stood there in my underwear while the gun got heavier and heavier. I didn't move or make a sound. When the waiting got hard I thought how hard it was for him, and then I knew I could wait all night if I had to.

But I didn't have to.

I didn't hear him approach. He was damned good. The first

sound I heard was a tentative scratching at the door, like a cat wanting to come in. Then my name repeated twice. Loud enough so I would hear it if I was awake, soft enough so that it would never wake me.

The key slipped in silently. He must have picked up an extra key when he signed us in, and he must have soaped it to muffle the sound. I listened to the lock turn.

Then, slowly, the door opened at me.

No shoes. He was fully clothed otherwise, but no shoes. The gun was in his right hand. It looked like a .22, and there was a silencer on the end of the barrel.

He walked all the way to the bed with the gun trained on my pillows, and I kept the Magnum on him every step of the way.

For a while I thought he was actually going to fire the gun. I was hoping he would, and it did look that way, but at the last moment something must have cued him. He kept the gun muzzle trained on the pillows and groped for the bedside lamp with his free hand.

It was really beautiful when the light went on.

All I saw was his back, but it was like watching a face change expression. He froze, and I looked at his back and saw thoughts going through his head. He knew exactly where I was. He knew I had a gun on him. He knew that his only hope was to spin around and shoot, and he also knew that there wasn't one chance in a thousand that he would make it. He thought of a lot of things to say, but none seemed better than silence, and he waited, and I let him wait.

I let him wait until it was too good, until I couldn't take any more of it.

Then I said, "Sometimes, George, you're a real moron."

SIXTEEN

"Put The Gun on the bed. Now turn around. You should see your face, George. Sit down on the floor. No, cross your legs, put your hands on your knees. Fine."

I closed the door, switched on the overhead light. I said, "I'll talk and you'll listen. Fair enough?"

He nodded.

"George, George. Once upon a time you told me that I was incompetent and untrustworthy, and now it looks as though you were describing yourself. You're both of those, all right," I sighed. "The best planner I've ever met in my life. Shrewd and cool and farsighted, and yet whenever I come into the picture something happens to your brain. You go out of your way to screw yourself up. I guess I'm your personal blind spot, George."

"I—"

"Uh-uh." I waggled the Magnum at him. "I talk and you listen, that's our arrangement. Or you get a new hole in your head. Agreed?"

He nodded.

"That's better. Oh, George, what the hell am I going to do with you? I knew all along you would try to kill me. Surprised? I started waiting for it from the minute the last of the soldiers was dead. I thought you might do it then and let Agent Lynch die with his faithful comrades, but you needed someone to drive the truck and help you tidy up.

"I was ready for you at the barn, too. It was such a natural spot, and you were all set, weren't you? Don't look as though you don't follow me. Come to think of it, try to keep your face as expressionless as possible. Don't talk, and don't make faces."

A nod.

"You were going to poison me. There were two bottles on the food table when we walked in, and the next time I looked there was only one, the Scotch. What was in the other one, water? You don't have to answer. Whatever it was, it was full of something fatal, but you decided to grant me a stay of execution. I wasn't bothering you, after all, and there was a lot of driving still to go, and suppose more snow fell and you had trouble getting out? I might come in handy." I shook my head. "Oh, George. Then you went and made a game out of it, the toast and all that. That's a bad habit of yours, you tend to overcompensate."

I paused, and he wanted to say something. He didn't dare. I stared at him and he kept his mouth shut.

"And I don't even have to tell you about tonight, do I? You telegraphed it all over the place. Even if I'd been as tired as I acted, I couldn't have missed it. 'Maybe we should stay out of Tampa. Where are we, anyway? Say, how about Savannah?' You're not supposed to let the bones show.

"The only part I couldn't figure was why. Why kill me? Because I might lead them to you? That might be a reason to kill me afterward, after the delivery was made. Or maybe a million isn't enough for you, maybe you want it all. Still, why rush things?" I shook my head. "No, there was only one thing I could think of, and then the stop in Savannah cinched it. The dirty stuff in the truck isn't going to our good-guy buddies. But I knew that all along, George. I knew that on the island."

His jaw dropped. Then his lips moved, but no sound came out.

"Oh, hell, you gave it away. You're easy to read, that's your trouble. Whenever you sell something too hard I know you're lying in your teeth. All that shit about how the stuff was getting to the right people after all. And the cutesy-pie chatter in Spanish, and dropping Tampa into every third sentence whether it fit or not. 'Look at the snow, Paulie, and I wonder how hot it is in Tampa.' Where are the goods going, George? What set of bad guys? Africa? The Middle East?" He hesitated. "You can answer the question. A special dispensation."

"Africa."

"Is that what you thought I wanted to hear? Because that's what you always tell me. We put nineteen men under the ground and jobbed the U.S. Army to hell and back, and you think I give a flying shit *where* the stuff goes? You really think that's how my head works? The ship's in Savannah instead of Tampa, and the buyers are baddies instead of goodies, and you think that would keep me up nights? It's annoying enough that you underestimate me twice an hour, George, but do you have to act as though I'm crazy, too?"

He studied his hands. I told him the speech was over and the floor was open for group discussion. He could talk if he wanted. He went on looking at his hands for a long time.

Then he said, "I made a mistake."

"Wonderful. It was my mistake letting you talk. 'I made a mistake.' You ought to have that tattooed on your ass. You damn fool, you've made ten mistakes a day."

"No. Just one. I read you wrong. Over and over and over. I had a fix on you before I went down to the Keys and you kept doing things to change my mind and I just wouldn't let you do it. Am I making sense?"

"Sure."

"I had this impression of you, I couldn't let go of it. I'm still having trouble breaking the habit. The weapons aren't going to Africa. There's this sheikdom on the Arabian Gulf—"

"I get the point."

"All right." He looked up. "I wish I had a cigarette."

"You quit."

"I know. Hell with it. I read you wrong, that's all. I never thought of killing you in South Dakota. In the barn, yes. The bottle was coffee laced with one of our new wonder drugs. I knew you'd want coffee. I was going to burn the barn down with you in it."

"What about here?"

"I would have put you in the van. They're loading it as a unit, they could have dropped you in the ocean. The ship's here in Savannah, of course. They load at noon, they ship out by one. Nice timing, huh?"

"Very nice. You were going to handle the deal yourself? You weren't afraid of a cross?"

"You mean by the buyers?" I nodded. "I thought of it. Not very seriously, but it did enter my mind. I think they'd rather pay the two million than lose a valuable contact. Oh, I knew you'd be insurance at the moment of exchange, but I had to pick the lesser of two evils."

"Next time toss a coin."

"I'll keep that in mind." His eyes narrowed suddenly. "I'm not telling you all this because confession is good for the soul. I already figured that you're not going to kill me." A shaky smile came and went. "If I called this one wrong, too—"

"No."

"Because if I did, then I deserve to die. No joke."

I shook my head. "Why kill you? Because you tried to kill me? The hell, I damn near drowned you twice before we even got started. I don't want to punish you. That's not my line. With you dead I'm out a million dollars. I want the money. I didn't do this for the money, not exactly, but now I want it. The only possible reason to kill you would be if you were still a threat to me. I don't think you are. It took you a while, but you're beginning to know who I am. I'm worth a lot more to you alive than dead, and so are you to me, so the hell with it."

He thought it all over. Then, slowly, he nodded.

"Go on back to your cabin. Knock yourself out with sleeping pills. We paid for the cabins, we might as well get some use out of them. We'll have a busy morning. You may trust your Arab buddies, but I don't. They may not realize you're worth more to them alive than dead. Sometimes even bright people make that mistake. Don't forget your gun. Go ahead, pick it up. We're big boys now. I'm not going to shoot you and you're not going to shoot me. And we both know it. Go get some sleep, George."

He walked out the door, took a few steps, stopped, turned. He said, "Paul? I wish this never happened and I'm glad it did. You follow? I'm glad you'll be in on it tomorrow. We might—who knows, we might even find things to do later on. When push comes to shove, we're not a bad team. Right?"

I told him to get the hell to bed.

It was his turn to wake up first. He woke me around eight. "I thought of holding a gun on you as a gag," he said. "But I figured you'd take it away from me and feed it to me through my ass."

"Probably."

"That's what I decided. Get dressed, we'll catch some breakfast."

We walked across the road to a diner. We ate a lot of eggs, drank a lot of coffee. We went back to my cabin. He had bought cigarettes at the diner, and he smoked one after another while he drew me a map of the Savannah docks.

I guess I must have reached him. He told me the whole play, and he knew I could have pushed him right then and finished the deal on my own, and he also knew I wouldn't. Progress.

I studied the map for a while. I said, "Okay, I've got it. Head into town, pick up a rental car. You'd better put on a suit. Bring the car here and we'll load what we need. Everything else does on the truck. Then you'll drive down to the wharves. You'll park—give me the map—you'll park here, and—''

We ran through it. He made a few suggestions, some good and some bad, and we played with it until it came out right. He headed off to rent a car. I opened up the back of the van, closed myself inside. I opened a few crates until I found what I wanted. I put a nuclear grenade and a launcher on the floor of the cab.

There was a shopping plaza next door to the diner. I went into a drugstore and bought two candy bars and a wind-up alarm clock. I got back before George. I stuck the alarm clock in the drawer and ate the candy bars. Then I took off the trucker duds, put on my suit, and put the trucking clothes on over it. I looked a little bulky, but no one was going to take my picture.

I was loading the truck when he brought the car around. It was a compact, either a Valiant or a Falcon, I never remember which is which. "All they had," he said. "It'll do, won't it?"

"Not if they pay off in singles."

"Probably fifties and hundreds."

"Then it'll do fine."

He offered to take the truck, but I said I would. He couldn't argue without looking as though he was pulling something, which was ridiculous, but he wasn't going to fight it. I told him to go on ahead, that I wanted the car parked and him in position before I took the truck out. He stopped to have a look at the grenade and launcher.

"Jesus," he said. "Sweet Jesus. Drive carefully, will you?"

"Nothing happens unless the pin is pulled."

"Maybe their quality control is spotty. Drive carefully anyway, huh?"

He took off. I finished putting our waste material in the van—his overalls, our jackets, a few odds and ends. I was going to keep the Magnum and shoulder rig, but at the last minute I added them, too. Once we made the trade I wouldn't need a gun, and meanwhile I had an atomic grenade, and it outranked the Magnum.

Then I went back for the alarm clock and climbed into the back of the van for the last time. I climbed back down a few minutes later, swept both of our cabins for prints—this last out of habit, there was no particular point to it. I stopped in at the office, but George had paid our tab in advance when we checked in.

I spent ten more minutes walking around the lot and taking big breaths. I hadn't really noticed it before, but it was a beautiful day. Blue sky and a sun. And, for the first time in too long, warmth. I hadn't realized just how much I'd missed it up there. Warmth. Heat from the sun.

I got up in the cab. I started the engine, flicked on the radio just in time for the news. Nothing. I killed the radio and made like a truckdriver.

His map was good. I only went wrong once, when a street I'd planned on taking turned out to be one-way the other way. I found a street that was going my way and drove straight to the waterfront, then headed directly for our pier. I had wondered what kind of a ship you could drive a full-size van onto, and now I knew. It was all alone out there and it was big. It was flying the Panamanian flag. If all those ships belonged to Panama, she could declare herself Mistress of the Seas. Or share the title with Liberia.

I wondered how fast boats like that went. It seemed to be the sort of thing a person ought to know, and I didn't have the vaguest idea.

I spotted the car. It was in position, tucked behind a shed and not visible from ship. I drove another couple dozen yards and braked to a stop. I opened the door, and George dashed out from cover. I slid over to let him behind the wheel.

He drove us out onto the pier. While they swung a ramp into position, I got out on my side and took the grenade and the launcher with me. I crouched on the pier with the truck shielding me. By the time George moved the van, I had the launcher sighted in and the grenade in place.

That was the end of my job. I didn't have anything else to do unless something was wrong. George was now telling them who I was and what I had aimed at them, and that it would blow them all to hell if he didn't get paid and set loose. If they shot me the grenade would be launched automatically. If they got very cute and shot the launcher out from under me, the grenade would blow on the spot; I was still close enough to take them with me.

Either they never planned a cross or he made it sound good, because he was walking off the ship past me in less than twenty minutes. He had two metal boxes, one in each hand. They looked like the kind that hold fishing tackle or plumber's tools, only larger. He didn't say anything; he just winked as he went by.

I waited until I heard his horn, one long, two shorts, one long. I backed off with the grenade launcher still pointing at the ship. That looked good, but I was afraid I'd fall over my own feet, so I gave up and turned around and walked the rest of the way with the launcher under my arm. I figured somebody had a gun on me all the way, and that he just might be addled enough to give the trigger a squeeze. But I got to the shed and turned the corner, and the car was there with the motor running and the door open on the passenger side. I hopped in, and we were moving before I could yank the door shut.

I separated the grenade and the launcher. I put the grenade in the glove compartment, chucked the launcher into the back seat.

He shuddered. "You had to bring them?"

"What did you want me to do with them?"

"I know. They make me nervous."

"We drove two thousand miles with a truck full of them, and now you're nervous."

"It's different. I just spent half an hour with this one pointed at me." He stuck a cigarette in his mouth and poked the dashboard lighter. He didn't say anything until he had treated his lungs to a cloud of smoke. Then he started giggling.

He said, "They never planned a cross. I'd give twenty-to-one on it. That bit with the grenade, they were terrified. Literally terrified. That you might slip. Anything."

"Just so they paid up. You couldn't have counted it."

"I had trouble enough lifting it. I gave it a quick check. All U.S., incidentally. I thought they might make up part of it in pounds, but it's nothing but dollars." He fell silent. He wasn't driving anywhere in particular, but he was making a lot of turns and keeping an eye on the mirror.

All at once he giggled again. "You missed a show," he said. "The boss man damn near had a stroke. 'What if your friend slips? What if zere iss an ox-see-dent?' To tell you the truth, the same thought occurred to me. That thing had me a little shaky."

"No need. I never engaged the pin."

He turned his head all the way around to look at me. "Truth?"

"Truth. I didn't want an ox-see-dent either."

"You could have told me."

"I figured you'd be more convincing this way. Sell the salesman, then let the salesman sell the product."

He thought about it. "I won't argue, friend Paul. As long as my hair isn't suddenly gray. Is it?"

"No."

"Then all is forgiven."

He got very jovial a few minutes later. I put myself into the mood and threw an arm over his shoulder. He started singing something. A college song, I think.

I moved my hand to the back of his neck. He stopped for a red light, and I used my thumb and forefinger on the big blood vessels on either side of his neck.

When the light changed, I was driving. He was on the passenger side, sound asleep.

SEVENTEEN

I WAS STANDING a few feet behind him when he came to. I had removed the gag once I had the boat a good ways out on the water, but I heard him fighting the ropes before he actually said anything. This went on for a few minutes, and I stopped what I was doing and watched. I had him on his back, wedged between the deck chair and the rail so he wouldn't roll around. His hands were tied behind his back with electrical wire. I had the same kind of wire wound around his legs in three places, and there was a heavy rope around his ankles.

He did all the squirming he could and proved that he wasn't going to accomplish anything that way. Then he stopped, and then he spoke in a whisper.

"Paul? Paul? Where are you, Paul?"

I said, "Here."

"I don't know how the hell they did it. Was it the Greek? The last thing I remember was driving, then nothing. We're on some kind of a boat. Not the *Pindaris*. Where are we?"

"The Atlantic. About four miles from land. International waters."

"Jesus, how did we—" He stopped short. "Paul?"

I walked around the deck chair on the port side. He didn't

say anything, and I watched his face as it all sank in. He got it a little at a time and his face kept on changing and he still didn't say a word.

"I rented the boat less than a mile down the waterfront from where we delivered the load. Did I say rented? I mean chartered. I chartered the ship. It's a cabin cruiser, sleeps four. A good-sized engine, but it's off now. We're drifting. Adrift in the Atlantic. I like the sound of that, don't you? Adrift in the Atlantic."

"I don't believe it."

"You will," I said. "There's loads of time. It's two o'clock, the *Pindaris* sailed an hour ago. I saw her leave. She's out of sight now. Pretty soon the sun will be over the yardarm. We don't have a yardarm, George. It's a nautical term. I don't know what it means."

"Is this a gag?"

"Guess."

"It might be your idea of a joke. We worked everything out, I made a mistake, a lot of mistakes, we worked everything out—"

"Uh-huh."

"It's not a joke," he said.

"No."

"You are going to kill me."

"Yes."

"For Christ's sake, why?" His voice was hoarse. "I'll never try to job you again, you must know that. Do you want the money? I can't believe it, but if you want it you can take it. Screw the money, I don't care about the money." A pause. "No, damn it, that's not it. I just don't believe it. That's not it, is it, Paul?"

"The money? No."

"Then—"

"I killed nineteen men for a million dollars. That's a little over fifty thousand dollars a man. If I killed you for another million I'd be cheapening their lives. It doesn't seem right."

He stared at me. "Oh, no. The one thing I never figured—"

"I got my million. Fair is fair. The other million is yours,
George. I wouldn't take it away from you."

"You snapped. You went over the edge. I never figured.
Paul, Paul—"

I dragged over one of the metal cases. I flipped the hinges,
lifted the lid. It was packed with fifty-dollar bills in stacks of
a hundred.

"See? A million dollars." I closed the box. "I don't want
it. Watch closely now, this is something you've never seen
before. Watch."

I threw the box over the side.

"I don't believe it."

I felt like singing. I knew I was smiling like an idiot but I
couldn't help it. "What's so hard to believe? There's too
much money in the world. Ordinarily I wouldn't throw it in
the ocean because the fish can't eat it. I only throw organic
refuse in the ocean. Sometimes, though, a man has to bend so
he won't break. Sometimes he can do both. A question of
compromise. The fish can't eat a grenade launcher—" I
threw the launcher over the side— "or a grenade—" I
flipped the grenade after it— "or the wires on your wrists, or
the rope around your ankles, or the anchor at the end of the
rope. If you lift your head you'll see the anchor. That's why
we're adrift in the Atlantic, George, not just for the beauty of
the phrase, the poetry of the words, but because the anchor is
here in the boat and you're attached to it. Are you getting
attached to your anchor, George? The fish won't eat it, or
your clothes, but they'll eat *you*, George!"

I started laughing and couldn't get hold of it. I grabbed
onto the rail and clenched my teeth and shut my eyes and took
deep breaths, in out in out. I knew what was happening. A
corner of my mind knew exactly what was happening, and I
kept my eyes shut and my jaws locked together and kept
taking deep breaths until the rough parts smoothed out again.

He was saying the same thing, over and over, as if the

words had magical properties. "You're crazy. You're out of your mind, you're crazy—"

I stood and watched him. I was calm now, and so of course he started to tell me that I had to calm down. "I think I'll go below," I told him. "That's another nautical term. It means downstairs. Try to get some rest, George."

I went downstairs and sat on a bed and wondered what they called beds on a ship. It wasn't going well, I told myself. I couldn't get organized, I kept going off on tangents and winding up hysterical. I had to straighten myself out. One thing at a time, one damned thing at a time.

I thought it all out and had it fixed in my mind when I went upstairs again. He was lying still, and for a moment I thought he was dead, but then his eyes turned to focus on me. He didn't say anything.

I said, "I want you to understand all this. It's almost 2:30 now. In an hour and a half, at four o'clock, the *Pindaris* will blow up. We may hear it, I'm not sure, I may, I mean. I don't know what speed a big ship makes or—"

"The *Pindaris* will—"

"Please don't interrupt. Let me talk, and then later you can ask all the questions you want, and I'll try to answer them. I think I knew all along that I was going to blow up the ship. I think that's one of the reasons I agreed to do the job in the first place. Those weapons are disgusting. They don't just kill people, they kill everything. Everything. They kill the ground."

"How did—"

"Please. You know the outfit I was in. We learned how to make bombs out of almost anything. I bought an alarm clock for the timer and opened up bullets for gunpowder. And other things. I set it all up while you were driving to the pier. In one of the crates I broke open. It won't be much of a bomb. A little explosion and a little fire, but the explosion alone ought to be enough to start some of the napalm, and once that goes it'll touch off most of the other stuff."

I took a deep breath. "Of course, blowing up the ship takes the pressure off us, too. Me. They'll know about it, that the weapons were destroyed, and it won't be quite as important to find out who took them. Maybe they'll decide that the criminals went down with the ship. So it's safer this way, but that's not the point, that's just a fringe benefit."

"A million dollars, a fortune in weapons, and a ship," he said. He was talking to himself. "I don't believe it. A ship, a freighter. I don't—"

I waited until he stopped. I was going to tell him that the only thing that really bothered me was the damage the blast would do: It would pollute a large portion of the sea and might disturb the ecology of the whole area. I didn't tell him because I knew he didn't care, and also because it was something I didn't want to think about myself. I would have to think about it sooner or later, but it could wait.

So I said, "I told you this because I had to, and it was something you had to know. But I know that you want to hear about yourself, don't you?"

"You already told me."

"Yes."

"You're going to dump me overboard."

"That's right."

He had a tremendous amount of control. I could almost see his mind trying to come apart, but he managed to keep it in check. He couldn't talk for a few minutes and I waited for him, and then he said, his voice steady, interested, "Why, Paul? *Why?*"

"Don't you know?"

"Because I tried to kill you."

"No. That would be stupid. I told you last night."

"Then why?"

I had had the right answer ready before but now I couldn't remember what it was. I hedged. "I'm safer this way. They might get to you, it's possible. And you would throw me to them, you know you would. Or else you would kill me yourself. I'd always be the loose end, the one man on earth who knew about you, and you would go to Guatemala and come back from Guatemala and think about me. You'd have a million dollars free and clear with one man in the world who knew about you, just one man, and it might take a month or a year or five years but sooner or later it would get to you and you would try to kill me."

"Never, Paul. Never."

"You would."

"Never, I swear it!"

It was a rotten trick and I was mad at myself. He had hope now. It was false hope, because he thought that was my real reason and that, since it was a rational reason, he could use reason to change my mind. He deserved to be treated as an equal. It was legitimate to hurt him, but this was not an honest way to do it.

The words rushed out of him. They were wasted, I couldn't even listen to them, but I let him go on. He never exactly finished. He ran out of breath, and when he did I held up a hand, and he let me talk.

"What I just said was true, don't interrupt, it was true, but that's not why I'm doing this." My head was splitting. I put my hand to my forehead and tried to hold it all together. "I want to tell you why. I want to, I want to tell you why, but there are too many reasons. I can't sort them out. Everything runs together."

"Paul—"

"You said I was crazy. No, no, wait, that didn't bother me. Don't you see? I know I'm crazy. But not just now, George. I've been crazy all along. My God, George, what do you expect? A guy cracks up and lives by himself on an island and runs around naked, of course he's crazy! What else would he be? You think he gets cured out there? Do you cure a lion by putting it in a cage?"

I stared into his eyes. He was beginning to understand. I think he was beginning to understand.

"You let the lion out of the cage," I told him. "I held the leash in my own hands and it worked, I stayed on the leash.

Sometimes it was close but it worked. But when the job was over the leash went away. Do you see? Do you see?''

He couldn't answer me.

"Why am I going to kill you? George, George, I have a hundred reasons. I have a million reasons. You came to my island. You went in my house. You read my list.'' I couldn't hold my voice down. It was getting louder and louder. "You threw a cigarette in the sand. Cellophane, the cellophane from the pack, you let it blow away. You watched me shoot the soldiers. You wouldn't do it yourself but you watched me do it.

"You talked to me! You made me break my rules! You made me talk to you, you made me want to break the rules! You take pills! You smoke! Damn you, you bastard, I already killed you. I drowned you and I could have left you in the water but I didn't. I made you dead and then I made you alive again, but you've been dead all along. That's why the boat, that's why it has to be drowning.''

"Paul, Paul—''

"You came too close! I made myself stop talking to people and you made me talk to you! I was free, I was alone, and you came close! I was alone and I was myself and you wrecked that, you pushed your way in and now you're me and I'm you! *You're the me I hate!*''

I stood there listening to that last sentence ringing in the air. It had come out all by itself. It was true, and it was a truth I hadn't known about before. I could feel tears behind my eyes. I knew they wouldn't flow, I knew it, but they were there.

I went downstairs again. Below. When I came back he said, "Paul, I give up. You don't want to torture me. End it.''

"Do it yourself.'' He didn't understand. "Take the black pill,'' I said. "You once told me I'd never do it. Neither will you. You've got a hollow tooth, I found it when I gagged you. Bite it, take the black pill. It's easier than drowning.''

He breathed. In and out, in and out.

''That's what I thought. Part of you keeps thinking I'll change my mind. That's what I thought, but I had to find out for sure. Even when you're under you'll wonder if I'm going to pull you back up and let you go. You'll keep on wondering, and then you'll drown. Again.''

''Paul—''

I didn't listen. I picked him up. I was surprised how easy he was to lift. He flapped like a fish, but he was still easy to lift. I wanted to make it fast now before something went wrong. I threw him overboard.

The fucking line was too short. He hung head downward, his head just a foot from the water surface, and he was screaming. I grabbed the anchor and heaved it after him, and by the time I looked he was gone.

At four o'clock I thought I heard a noise, a rumbling noise far out to sea. I went to the rail but I couldn't see anything. It could very well have been thunder, a storm out over the Atlantic. Or my imagination.

EIGHTEEN

I DON'T KNOW how long I stayed on the boat. For a few days I left the engines off and stayed adrift in the Atlantic. The boat became a surrogate for my island, but without the discipline. There was food and water on board. I drank water, but as far as I know I didn't touch the food. I think I slept a lot, but all the edges of memory are blurred, and I could not say what happened and what was dream.

This did happen: one night I took off all my clothes and jumped overboard and swam out to sea, away from the ship. I may have meant to drown myself, but it could also have been a test, a game. If so, I proved what I had set out to prove, and thus lost or won, as you prefer. I couldn't take black pills either. Somehow I swam back to the ship and managed to drag myself aboard.

That must have been a turning point, or the signal of a turning point, because the next thing I did was start the engines. I set out to run the boat south, and figured that I could stay within sight of the coast and cruise all the way around Florida to my island.

Madness has many phases. This phase was good enough to wear off before the tanks ran dry. I suddenly realized one day that I would run out of fuel and be permanently adrift in the Atlantic, and the phase instantly lost its charm.

I docked at a private marina outside of Neptune Beach, which is a shore suburb of Jacksonville. It was the middle of the night and no one was around, and I tied up my boat like a good little sailor and walked through the grounds unchallenged. Pure dumb luck, and it got me through the most genuinely hazardous part of the whole operation. There I was with no identification, someone else's boat, and a million dollars in a metal satchel. I didn't even realize the danger until it was long past.

The time on the boat established one thing. By the time I got off it I knew that all the things I had to do would have to wait until I was in shape to do them. Buying the land, stashing the money, everything. None of it was that goddamned urgent. It could wait. First I had to go home.

I sat in a Turkish bath in Jax until the barbershops opened. I went to one and got a shave and a haircut. A Chinese laundryman pressed my suit while I waited. Then I walked over to the terminal and got on a bus.

He didn't recognize me. He pointed his eyes at the middle of my chest, and he put the cracker accent on hard, the way he'll do with mainland types.

I said, "I'll bet you forgot the dictionary, too."

The eyes jumped, the mouth gaped. "Now I will be damned," he said. "Now I will be paternally damned. Do you know I didn't *know* you? By God, I don't know as I can be blamed. No beard, next to no hair, and pale enough to pass for white." He suddenly remembered that the radio was on and that it was against my religion. He spun around and turned it off, then turned to face me again.

"A dozen aigs and what-all else? You know, I never thought I'd get to say that again." His face turned serious.

"Thought I'd gone and lost your trade. Thought you were dead, if I'm damned for saying it. Been how long? A month?"

"About that."

"Haven't been sick, have you?"

"Up North."

"About the same, some would say." He leaned on the counter. "Well, now."

I didn't want to be too talkative, but I had to fill in a few blanks for him. "Sudden trip," I said. "A boat came across from Little Table Key to pick me up."

"Business?"

"A death."

"Oh, now," he said. "I am sorry. Kin of yours?"

"A friend," I said. "My only really close friend."

"Terrible. A young fellow, I suppose."

"About my age."

"Terrible. Sudden?"

I thought for a moment. "No," I said finally. "No, not sudden. We knew it was coming. It was just a question of when."

I told him I would hold off on restocking until I had a chance to take inventory. I explained that my own rowboat was on the island and he immediately offered to run me over. I said I'd just as soon go myself, if he knew where I could borrow a boat; I'd tow it back tomorrow or the day after. He had a dinghy with an outboard on it and said I could keep it as long as I wanted.

"And one thing you don't walk off without, by God." He reached under the counter, pulled out a book and slapped it down hard. It was a paperback dictionary. "That's a bet you just lost, that I wouldn't remember it. Oh, and there's a story goes with it."

He propped himself up on his elbows, grinning at the memory. "That fellow brought the dictionary, you know, and he always just goes and sets the books in the rack and clears out the old ones. Well, the wife was here at the time and of course she didn't even think. And a couple of days go by, see, and this nigra comes in. Suit and a tie and you just knew he walked through life waiting for someone to take his photograph. Well, what does he pick out but the dictionary.

"Now you can imagine. First time in the store, and he brings this book over to the counter, and what do I have to say? 'Oh, can't sell you that, it's reserved on special order.' Which is exactly the truth, and I'd of had a better chance of convincing this nigra that I'm a bleached Chinaman myself, see? And the more I talk the madder he gets, and I just keep on explaining and explaining. 'Take another book, take a dozen.' I tell him. 'Have a Coke, free, my compliments, drink it right here in the store, hell, I'll get you my own damn *glass*.' And out he goes with his nose scraping the ceiling."

He cackled. "So of course for the next three days I sat and worried about it. Every morning I woke up looking to see a picket line around the house with Martin Luther Coon himself at the head of it. You wouldn't believe the thoughts went through my mind, and of course I never heard any more about it, or saw that particular son of a bitch again, and doubtless never will. But that's your dictionary, and it's been in back of this counter ever since, and it's marked sixty cents and cost me thirty-six, and it is yours free like the Coke the nigra wouldn't take, because if I didn't get thirty-six *dollars* worth of excitement out of it I don't know what."

And out back, when he showed me the boat, he said. "I hate to tell you this but I'd hate worse to go without. About two weeks ago I took a liberty. I went out to your island." He turned his face away. "I thought it over and thought it over, and the wife said either you were dead and couldn't be helped or alive and wouldn't welcome company, but all I could think of is what if you were sick? So I took the boat around just for a look and saw *your* boat on the beach, and I thought, well, he isn't gone anywhere, and then I saw all this weed and such on the beach, and called to you and couldn't raise you, and that's when I worried.

"I went ashore and just checked to see if you were about. I went close enough to the shack to see inside, but I swear I never set foot in the door or touched nothing. Then I thought, well, he must of drowned, and came back."

I didn't say anything. He turned to look at me. "It was a liberty, and it won't happen again."

"Oh, now. You were doing me a kindness."

"I hope you'll think so." He snapped quickly out of the mood. "Well, now, you keep that dinghy long as you like, hear? And next time you come I'll have that dozen aigs—"

The beach was a mess. I started to pick things up but there was too much debris and too many things to do first.

I got out of my clothes. They had been comfortable all along, but as soon as I set foot on my island they felt as though they were strangling me. Eventually I would decide whether any of them was worth keeping.

I carried the metal satchel half the length of the island. I dug a hole alongside a sick-looking palm tree and buried the box under three feet of sand.

I went to my other burying place and dug up the aluminum-foil packet. I opened it, and to the bills inside it I added my money belt and the large bills from my wallet. I kept the smaller bills and change handy for trips to Mushroom Key, and I carried my *Do Nothing* list back to the shack. I read it aloud and tacked it in place on the inside of the door. Then I read it through a second time, and only then did I go back to cover up my money belt and smooth the sand over it.

I ran one lap around the island. Ritual, perhaps; the animal staking out his territory. My wind was bad but it wouldn't take long to improve it. I caught my breath, and then I ran out into the sea and swam around. I stayed in the water for quite a while. Then I came out and sprawled face down in the sand with the hot sun on my back.

Vacations are fun, but they're right. The best part is getting home again.

FINE MYSTERY AND SUSPENSE TITLES FROM CARROLL & GRAF

☐ Allingham, Margery/MR. CAMPION'S FARTHING	$3.95
☐ Allingham, Margery/MR. CAMPION'S QUARRY	$3.95
☐ Allingham, Margery/NO LOVE LOST	$3.95
☐ Allingham, Margery/THE WHITE COTTAGE MYSTERY	$3.50
☐ Ambler, Eric/BACKGROUND TO DANGER	$3.95
☐ Ambler, Eric/CAUSE FOR ALARM	$3.95
☐ Ambler, Eric/A COFFIN FOR DIMITRIOS	$3.95
☐ Ambler, Eric/EPITAPH FOR A SPY	$3.95
☐ Ambler, Eric/STATE OF SIEGE	$3.95
☐ Ambler, Eric/JOURNEY INTO FEAR	$3.95
☐ Ball, John/THE KIWI TARGET	$3.95
☐ Bentley, E.C./TRENT'S OWN CASE	$3.95
☐ Blake, Nicholas/A TANGLED WEB	$3.50
☐ Brand, Christianna/DEATH IN HIGH HEELS	$3.95
☐ Brand, Christianna/GREEN FOR DANGER	$3.95
☐ Brand, Christianna/FOG OF DOUBT	$3.50
☐ Brand, Christianna/TOUR DE FORCE	$3.95
☐ Brown, Fredric/THE LENIENT BEAST	$3.50
☐ Brown, Fredric/MURDER CAN BE FUN	$3.95
☐ Brown, Fredric/THE SCREAMING MIMI	$3.50
☐ Browne, Howard/THIN AIR	$3.50
☐ Buchan, John/JOHN MACNAB	$3.95
☐ Buchan, John/WITCH WOOD	$3.95
☐ Burnett, W.R./LITTLE CAESAR	$3.50
☐ Butler, Gerald/KISS THE BLOOD OFF MY HANDS	$3.95
☐ Carr, John Dickson/CAPTAIN CUT-THROAT	$3.95
☐ Carr, John Dickson/DARK OF THE MOON	$3.50
☐ Carr, John Dickson/THE DEMONIACS	$3.95
☐ Carr, John Dickson/FIRE, BURN!	$3.50
☐ Carr, John Dickson/THE GHOSTS' HIGH NOON	$3.95

☐ Carr, John Dickson/NINE WRONG
ANSWERS $3.50
☐ Carr, John Dickson/PAPA LA-BAS $3.95
☐ Carr, John Dickson/THE WITCH OF THE LOW
TIDE $3.95
☐ Chesterton, G. K./THE MAN WHO KNEW TOO
MUCH $3.95
☐ Chesterton, G. K./THE MAN WHO WAS
THURSDAY $3.50
☐ Coles, Manning/ALL THAT GLITTERS $3.95
☐ Coles, Manning/THE FIFTH MAN $2.95
☐ Coles, Manning/THE MAN IN THE GREEN
HAT $3.50
☐ Coles, Manning/NO ENTRY $3.50
☐ Collins, Michael/WALK A BLACK WIND $3.95
☐ Crofts, Freeman Wills/THE CASK $3.95
☐ Crofts, Freeman Wills/INSPECTOR FRENCH'S
GREATEST CASE $3.50
☐ Dewey, Thomas B./THE MEAN STREETS $3.50
☐ Dickson, Carter/THE CURSE OF THE BRONZE
LAMP $3.50
☐ Disch, Thomas M & Sladek, John/BLACK
ALICE $3.95
☐ Eberhart, Mignon/MESSAGE FROM HONG
KONG $3.50
☐ Eastlake, William/CASTLE KEEP $3.50
☐ Farrell, Henry/WHAT EVER HAPPENED TO
BABY JANE? $3.95
☐ Fennelly, Tony/THE CLOSET HANGING $3.50
☐ Freeling, Nicolas/LOVE IN AMSTERDAM $3.95
☐ Freeman, R. Austin/THE EYE OF OSIRIS $3.95
☐ Freeman, R. Austin/MYSTERY OF ANGELINA
FROOD $3.95
☐ Freeman, R. Austin/THE RED THUMB
MARK $3.50
☐ Gardner, Erle Stanley/DEAD MEN'S LETTERS $4.50
☐ Gilbert, Michael/ANYTHING FOR A QUIET
LIFE $3.95
☐ Gilbert, Michael/THE DOORS OPEN $3.95
☐ Gilbert, Michael/THE 92nd TIGER $3.95
☐ Gilbert, Michael/OVERDRIVE $3.95

☐ Waugh, Hillary/A DEATH IN A TOWN $3.95
☐ Waugh, Hillary/LAST SEEN WEARING $3.95
☐ Waugh, Hillary/SLEEP LONG, MY LOVE $3.95
☐ Westlake, Donald E./THE MERCENARIES $3.95
☐ Willeford, Charles/THE WOMAN CHASER $3.95
☐ Wilson, Colin/A CRIMINAL HISTORY OF
    MANKIND $13.95